ECHOES
from the
INFANTRY

★

Frank Nappi

★

ECHOES
from the
INFANTRY

★

A NOVEL

St. Martin's Press

New York

www.stmartins.com

Design by Kathryn Parise

LIBRARY OF CONGRESS CATALOGING-IN-PUBLICATION DATA

Nappi, Frank.
    Echoes from the infantry: a novel / Frank Nappi.—1st ed.
       p.   cm.
    ISBN 0-312-33272-6
    EAN 978-0-312-33272-3
    1. World War, 1939–1945—Veterans—Fiction.   2. World War,
1939–1945—Fiction.   3. Long Island (N.Y.)—Fiction.   4. Fathers
and sons—Fiction.   5. Soldiers—Fiction.   I. Title.

PS3614.A664E27   2005
813'.6—dc22

                                                      2005046590

First Edition: November 2005

10   9   8   7   6   5   4   3   2   1

Dedicated to Mr. Edward Hynes, Mr. Bill McGinn,
and all of the World War II infantry soldiers who eluded
the cold hand of death but remained mired
in the psychological cloud of combat

The soldier, above all other people,
    prays for peace,
for he alone must suffer and bear the
deepest wounds and scars of war.

—GENERAL DOUGLAS MACARTHUR

ECHOES

from the

INFANTRY

★

PROLOGUE

✫

Being in the house after Madeline's death is strange for all of them. It has been almost two months, and James is no better. John flies in on a red-eye from California to be with his brothers and agrees to stay until they decide what to do about their father.

They stay in their old rooms, haunted by the old smells and sounds. Thoughts of their mother weigh heavily on their minds. They do not sleep much. When they do finally drift off, the barking dog next door brings them right back.

In the morning they awake and scarcely remember having slept at all. They sit at the kitchen table. The smell of coffee billows from Dunkin' Donut cups. They talk across linoleum squares that are scratchy with powdered sugar and bagel crumbs. James is by himself, seated quietly in his chair by the window.

Sitting in the old house, the way they used to, raises a flood of memories. They laugh. Matthew begins the jaunt through the past: teachers they shared, unusual hobbies they pursued, old girlfriends. They torture each other with secrets that have never been told and with vivid descriptions of some of the more embarrassing moments from their earlier years.

"Hey Johnny, do you remember that time we took Paul to get a haircut?" Matthew muses.

John begins to laugh, the first time he has as much as smiled since he got there.

"Ha, ha, ha," Paul mocks. "You guys were hilarious."

"What?" Matthew inquires innocently. "Mom told us to take you to Ozzie's for a haircut. That's what we did. Was it our fault he shaved your head?" He winks at John.

"Don't think I don't know you guys told him to," Paul says.

"I know something else too," he continues. "Neither one of you assholes would have survived a day in this house as the youngest!"

John yawns and rubs his eyes. "I never thought that goddamn dog would stop barking last night. I was up for hours."

"Yeah, I heard it too," Matthew says. "But it made me laugh. I couldn't stop thinking of the Eckers' dog. What was his name again?"

"Duke," Paul adds.

"Yeah, that's it. Now, there's a blast from the past. Remember those tape-ball games?"

"Yeah," Matt recalls, snickering at images from long ago.

"Boy, Johnny, you sure were stupid. How many times did we get you with that?"

"What do you mean?" he protests, embarrassed by the memory. "I knew what you guys were doing every time."

"Yeah, sure you did. That's not the way I remember it. Perhaps we should refresh your memory a little."

Paul and Matt begin talking about Mr. Ecker's fence, a six-foot metal barrier with multiple strips of green and white aluminum woven through the chain links. It was their home-run fence for the duration of their childhood. It stood about one hundred feet away from the home plate they had set up by the curb across the street. Over the years, not many of the balls they fashioned from stray rolls of masking tape managed to clear the top bar of the green and white wall. The contact with the plastic bat had to be perfect, and the wind needed to be blowing in just the right direction. Now and then, however, everything came together, and the little tan ball whistled by their ears and sailed up and out of the makeshift ballpark.

The celebration for the one responsible was dubious at best. The rule that they had established was simple: the person who hit the ball over the fence was the one who had to retrieve it.

Scaling the six-foot barrier wasn't nearly as perilous as what lurked behind it—a tall, sleek Doberman Pinscher named Duke. Duke was a legend on their street. All the kids in the neighborhood told stories about the dog: children who wandered into his yard, never to be seen again; a mailman whose indiscretion resulted in his leg being severed from the knee down. Then, when Mr. Ecker's wife took ill and nobody had seen her for months, there was the insidious rumor that Duke had actually run amok through the house and swallowed her whole.

The stories were endless, and the children believed every one of them. Duke was the most ill-tempered animal they had ever known. Even walking on the sidewalk that flanked the Eckers' property was unnerving. The slightest sound along the perimeter of the fence launched Duke into a dizzying fit of malevolence that sent the hair on the back of their necks straight up.

"Just how many balls *did* you hit over that fence, Johnny?" Matt asks. They all laugh.

John is the oldest and the strongest. Naturally, he holds the honor of having hit the most balls into the Eckers' yard. He also is the one who has had the most encounters with Duke.

On those rare occasions when the ball did sail over the fence, there was a "waiting period" before any attempt at a rescue could be made. Duke was vicious, but he lacked stamina. After a few minutes of barking and growling, the bilious beast always tired and retreated to another part of the yard. This was the signal to begin.

John would begin to climb the fence, painfully aware that the slightest sound would summon Duke from somewhere in the yard. Once safely inside, timing became paramount. Find the ball. Get out as fast as you could. These were the keys to surviving long enough to see another game.

Matthew and Paul always stood on the other side of the fence. They were the sentinels of the group. They would watch quietly from the safe side of the fence while their brother negotiated the other.

"Tell me if he's coming," John always reminded them.

"Okay," they would whisper back.

Then they would follow his every step, holding their breath as he inched his way past lawn sprinklers and rubber dog toys en route to the coveted prize, well aware that the fate of their play was suspended at some unknown point beyond the great green and white barrier.

When the ball was finally found, John would begin walking back across the yard, pleased that he had survived another date with Duke. But the devil inside his brothers always surfaced right about then, and before John knew what was happening, they were banging the fence with the plastic bat, and John was cursing them, Duke snapping at his heels. They always promised they would never do it again, but every time John hit the ball over the fence, they couldn't help themselves.

John listens as his brothers laugh and guffaw. He frowns. They would always catch trouble once they got home.

"Jonathan! Mrs. Ecker called again," James said from behind his newspaper. "Stay out of that goddamned yard, once and for all!"

"Serves you right, Johnny," Paul says, "for hitting all those home runs."

The distant but audible sound of James's sighs brings them back to the matter at hand. John motions to the chair where James remains seated.

"What are we gonna do with him, Pauly? Is this what he's like all the time?"

"I told you on the phone, John. It's bad."

"Well, he obviously can't stay here anymore. He's a danger to himself. And what are the rest of us supposed to do, come running every time he falls down or forgets to wash himself? I won't do that."

"Jesus, Johnny, keep your voice down," Matthew interrupts. "He's upset. Depressed. He's not deaf."

"Listen, all I'm saying is that the best thing for us—and him—is to put him in a home of some sort. He'll be safe there."

"Hey, wait a minute. We never said anything about a home, Johnny."

"Pauly's right, Johnny. That was never even a consideration."

"Well, what did you think we were going to do? Boy, you two are a couple of princes. All of a sudden we're sentimental and understanding. What a crock of shit. I'll tell you one thing: he's not coming back to California with me."

"Hey listen," Paul interrupts. "If I had to I could always make the room. It would be a bit of an inconvenience, but if it's the only way . . ."

"The old man belongs in a home. That's where men like him go. Why is that so hard to understand?"

"It's not the only way," Matt interrupts, ignoring his older brother. "Look. I have the room at my place. He can move in with me temporarily. We'll see how it goes. If it's not working out, then we can talk about a home."

John walks to the counter and bangs his mug in the sink.

"What the hell is going on here? Why are you guys fighting me?" His eyes dart wildly between his brothers.

"Man, what the hell is your problem, Johnny?" Matt says. "The misunderstood-wayward-son routine is getting a little tired. You're not the only one who feels cheated here."

Matt's outburst strikes a chord.

"I don't have to answer to you," John snaps back. "I came out here to help. That's all. I really don't give a shit what you do. In a couple of days, the garbage will be piled up on the curb, and I'll be on a plane back home."

"Yeah, isn't that just the way it's always been," Paul says. "You go off and do your thing, take care of yourself, and leave the rest of us holding the bag."

"What the hell are you talking about?" John says. "I'm here, aren't I?"

"Okay, then it's all settled," Matthew says. "We can get started cleaning out the house right away. It could be on the market by the end of the week. One less headache for all of us."

"Yeah, but how are we going to get all of this stuff moved out in a week?" Paul asks.

"No problem, Pauly," John answers. "You and Matt go to work today like you planned. Dad can stay here with me. I'll do as much as I can. Then, after work, you can swing by and give me a hand. We'll be done in no time."

John begins shortly after they leave. He climbs the stairs to the attic. The smell of mildew on wood greets him immediately. It is an attic like most, a treasure trove of junk and mementos from times long since past.

His feet move gingerly across the creaky floorboards to a wall stacked with cardboard boxes. As he moves, he passes by scattered artifacts that collectively tell the story of his life.

He removes the dusty lid from a white hat box filled with family photographs that have slept quietly for years beneath his grandmother's sewing machine. He reaches inside, removes some of the pictures, and glances nostalgically at the assorted scenes from his past: his first Holy Communion, the sixth-grade class trip to the Bronx Zoo, high school graduation. He opens his fist and lets the memories cascade back into the box.

Across the way are more treasures: Madeline's wedding dress, the hand-carved rocking horse his parents purchased from a tiny shop in Upstate New York when he was just a baby,

Grandma McCleary's wooden crib, the doorjamb he did not know his mother saved, complete with pencil marks charting the growth of all three McCleary boys at various times in their lives. He could still hear the sound of their young, eager voices clamoring for the tape measure and pencil. "It's my turn, Mommy! Measure me! Measure me!"

He finds other items that conjure much less pleasant recollections. In a milk crate next to a tiny plastic piano he uncovers a pair of sandals and a frayed poncho. The discovery takes him right back to the summer of his eighteenth year.

It was a warm July night. He was drinking down at the beach with his friends. The smell of marijuana lingered in the air; many of the defiant teens sat in a circle and shared their drugs and views on politics and war. Somewhere between the volleyball game and skinny-dipping, he lost his car keys. It was of little consequence, he thought. He only lived about two miles away.

When he arrived home, some of the stupor had lifted and he realized that he did not have a key to his house either. He tried the front window, but it was sealed shut by countless coats of paint applied carelessly over the years. "Shit!" he screamed in anger.

He crossed the lawn, heading toward the window on the side of the house. But before he could get there, the front door swung open. It was his father. He stood in the doorway, staring at him. He looked him up and down, from the long, snarled hair that hung down in his face to the brown sandals on his feet. John looked back at him, waiting to be admonished. He was ready for the confrontation. He wanted it. James just turned his back and walked upstairs.

He remembers how two weeks later he moved out, left for

college in California. His father barely said anything to him that afternoon too.

The move worked out well for him. It was there on campus he met his wife, Michele, and it was there he made friends with the son of the president of a German company that manufactures radios for distribution all over the world. He boasts to his brothers all the time about the benefits of working for a foreign company, including the many trips to Germany he has made and how proficient he has become in the language. "I'm an international man of intrigue," he always tells them with a smile.

The attic is also filled with many things about which John knows nothing. Old black-and-white photographs of faces he has never seen; empty wine bottles, old greeting cards, and other remnants of celebrations past: his father's army footlocker, a dusty green chest filled with military paraphernalia.

He looks quickly, having little interest in the war. He sorts through the shirts, pants, and boots. In addition to two canteens and some medallions, he finds a bunch of photographs lying inside a helmet and a field pack. The pictures depict his father and his friends. His father looks very different. He saves the pictures but tosses the pack aside.

When he has seen enough, he crosses to another part of the attic and crouches in front of a rose-colored shoe box with the initials M. A. B. printed neatly on the top. He opens the lid. There are many letters tied together with a piece of red yarn. They are all addressed to his mother. He untangles the knot and opens the one on top. He reads.

The first one is dated July 7, 1944. It begins with a description of the coastline in France and details the hardships of the voyage over. It is written on American Red Cross stationery. The handwriting is impeccable, but some of it has been blackened out. Still, there is enough to hold his interest.

The voice is one he does not recognize; it is human, warm, and full of hope and love and fear and uncertainty. The words are so heartfelt and so compelling that he skips to the other side of the page to see who it is from. On the bottom of the wrinkled paper is his father's name.

He repeats the process with each of the letters, only to discover the same thing. His knees, weak and tired from crouching, are bothering him. He sits on the dusty top of an old table, flips back to the first letter, and begins to read.

ONE

✴

Madeline came home to find James on the couch. She set her bags down and kissed his cheek. He was unavailable. He reminded her somehow of those German cities in ruin: not functioning and only remotely hopeful for a future.

"My goodness, the stores were mobbed," she said. "I've never seen anything like it."

He barely acknowledged her arrival. He was lost in the familiar practice of stuffing those goddamned socks under his arm. Those socks. How she hated those socks. More than anything. More than the way he sat in the living room of their home in the evenings, staring vacantly out the window into the darkness; more than the way he jumped to attention each time an airplane passed overhead or a car door slammed. Those socks. He had them squirreled away in every room. There were enough pairs to outfit all the New York Yankees. They were more disconcerting than the way he ground his teeth while he slept or the way his mind drifted during moments such as these.

She had tried. From the moment he came back to Rockaway, she tried to guide him gently toward his new life. She prepared all of his favorite meals. She made certain that the house was always warm. Fresh flowers adorned the tables in each room, and the soothing tones of classical piano insulated their home from the harsh sounds of the street, which always seemed to bring him back to the front line.

"Jimmy!" she admonished him. "Did you hear a word I just said?"

Her arms were folded. The tapping of her foot on the oak floor echoed like a drumroll.

"Yeah, yeah, Maddie. I heard you." He pulled his hand out from under his shirt. His gaze was still off in the other direction.

"Look, Jimmy. This has gone on long enough," she said. "It's time to live again. Time to be a husband again. Jimmy, please. Put those damn socks away."

They were the most difficult words she had ever spoken. She labored for weeks over how and when and even if she should. He was unpredictable and at times volatile, particularly when she questioned the reason behind what he was doing. This fear had held her voice captive. Until now.

When she heard the words leave her lips, she was surprised, almost as if they were uttered by someone else.

"What did you say?" he responded, cutting her down with his icy stare. "Why would you ask me that?"

She cowered in front of him like a frightened child. She did not answer. Why had she said anything? She should have kept her mouth closed, left him to his thoughts. Now she was reeling, and with nothing else to say, her silence enraged him. He grabbed her by the wrists and shook her violently, muttering something about soldiers and shell holes and Bastogne in the winter. She started to cry. He released her abruptly and stormed upstairs, leaving her crumpled on the floor.

She had bundled up his uniforms and his pack, buried them in his footlocker and tucked it all away neatly in a corner of the attic. She had hidden his souvenir weapons and photographs as well. Even the decorations he had received were placed out of his reach, in the back of her jewelry box. She thought she had covered everything, separated him from the world that still haunted him. But she had forgotten something.

She sat on the floor, feeling stupid and childish. Dusk had crept through the windows, and there she sat, crying, wiping her eyes on her shirt sleeves. She did not want to feel this way. It was worse than any confrontation with James could ever be. She lifted herself off the floor, grabbed a bag, and gathered every last pair of socks he had, leaving only the ones under his armpit and on his feet. She found him upstairs, sitting in the shadows of their bedroom, his head resting in the palms of his hands.

"Jimmy," she whispered. "I don't know exactly why you are still carrying those socks. I'm sure you have a good reason. But you're home now. You don't need them, sweetheart."

She ran her hand gently across her protruding belly. There wasn't going to be room for an extra pair of socks in the life Maddie had planned for herself and for her family. There were things now more important than socks, something inside of her, a new life, full of hope and promise. He needed to understand that.

"Let me have them, Jimmy. Please. I want them."

He rose slowly but said nothing. He slid his hands around her waist and locked them behind her back. Then he started to crumble.

"I'm sorry, Maddie. I'm sorry. But I can't. I can't do it," he said, choking on every word. "I can't do it, Maddie."

He buried his face in her neck and sobbed. She embraced him, then pushed him away just far enough to look into his eyes.

"You have to, Jimmy. We are starting over here. And it can not wait."

His face softened. He unfastened the top two buttons on his shirt and removed the socks from under his right arm. He handed them to her.

"Thank you, sweetheart," she said, drying his eyes with the last pair before dropping them into a bag with the others.

Afterward, they lay together, like weary travelers, stretched across the rumpled bed. In the darkness it was quiet, only the sweet smell of Madeline's perfume and his thoughts to keep him from losing himself in this new life. She turned on her side; her breath was warm against his ear. She was close to him; he could feel her breast, soft against his shoulder. His eyes remained closed as her hands moved over his chest and down his arms. With each pass of her palms she inched her face closer to his and with the gentleness of a hummingbird, began to pepper his cheek and neck with quiet kisses.

James was still, lost in the daunting words spoken only moments before: *Time to be a husband again.* He wasn't quite sure what that meant, or entailed. Did it mean providing for her and this family that was on the way? Or cutting the grass and putting snow tires on the car every winter? He could do all that. But what about everything else? What about moments like this, when it was just the two of them, naked before the light of truth? Would he ever be comfortable?

"Just relax, Jimmy," she said, listening to the irregular cadence of his breathing while stroking his face with her fingertip. "Everything is going to be great. We're going to be great."

Maybe she was right. Everything *would* be great. He could do this. Husband. Father. Plenty of guys did it. Why not him? He turned to her and opened his eyes. Her face was just a silhouette, glinting in the sheen of the moonlight. He pressed his mouth against hers. It was great. Everything would be great, he thought, if he could find a way to just forget.

TWO

✫

The town of Carentan was ordinary enough, with dirt roads and barren fields. But the sounds and smells were anything but familiar. They heard shots off in the distance, and the odor of sulfur was heavy in the air. They were a lot closer to the front than James had expected. He looked around and found physical reminders that he was not home anymore: winding miles of flowering orchards enclosed in hedgerows, the like of which he had never seen before. He was still trying to reconcile the image in his head when, next to the dirt road they followed, he saw the body of an American soldier lying on his side. He wondered how he got there and how he was killed. His right hand was resting quietly over his heart, and the other was stretched at his side, floating in a tiny puddle of mud.

James stopped and stared. His eyes moved over the outline of the dead soldier. The man's neck was cocked awkwardly, as if he were straining to hear something off in the distance. His eyes were open, and little green flies had found his mouth. His face was smooth, and his hands looked like they belonged to a student or writer. Both of his legs were twisted, and his left boot hung from his foot. They were the same boots James was wearing. The pack was also the same. So was the uniform, except for some words that peeked out from under the quiet hand. James knelt down next to the body and slid the hand away, revealing the mantra "Never Say Die" inscribed in black ink across the breast of the dead man's field jacket. He ran his fingers across his own chest as he read the words. At once he heard voices— Madeline's, his mother's, and several others from home—all struggling against the *ping-ping* of the cold raindrops hitting the top of his helmet. They were calling to him to be careful. They were reminding him of all he had to live for.

He heard Sergeant Billings, his drill instructor from Fort McCoy.

"Asses down, gentlemen. Make love to Mother Earth. A dirty soldier is a live soldier. Anyone here gets shot in the ass, I swear to God I'll finish the job myself."

Then he heard another voice. Peter Swinton's. "Come on, McCleary," he said. "Let's go do this thing."

Captain Peter Swinton had dark, sunken eyes and a crooked jaw. His voice, deep and raspy, made it even more difficult to listen to his proselytizing about army regulations. He was the el-

dest of six children born to Stanley and Claire Swinton of Fair-
field, Connecticut. Stanley's untimely death made ten-year-old
Petey an adult much sooner than Nature had intended. All of
his dreams and reckless aspirations were destroyed by the sudden call to duty.

When his mother was forced to exchange the role of homemaker for that of breadwinner, Swinton became the man of the
house. His brothers and sisters were his charges, and he accepted the role with the poise and dignity of one twice his age.
Even though he was only two years older than the rest of them,
they called him "Gramps" in recognition of his overriding commitment to all things practical.

Swinton was a military tactician. Everything was executed to
the letter. He was the kind of guy who would slam the proverbial round peg in the square hole if he thought that's what the
military wanted. He had great difficulty operating outside de-
lineated parameters.

At Fort McCoy, James and the others sat through weeks of
lectures on the most banal topics, ranging from "care of your
piece" to guard duty. Guard duty. That was Swinton's favorite.

"You will be protecting United States Army equipment gentlemen, and United States Army lives," he said, preening in
front of them like a rooster working a henhouse. "If you fail to
conduct yourselves in the manner in which you've been instructed, and there are any losses, equipment or personnel, you
will answer to me."

The very first time James was assigned to guard the entrance
to the facility, he was given explicit instructions.

"McCleary!" Swinton barked. "Nobody, I mean nobody,

gains entrance to this compound without giving the password. Nobody!"

"But sir," James answered. "Beg your pardon, but isn't the colonel expected today, sir?"

"What is your point, McCleary?"

"Sir, I don't want to insult the Colonel by asking him for a password."

"You will do as you're told, McCleary, damn you! Follow the general's orders. Like I do. Is that clear?"

James was not there more than an hour when off in the distance the wheels of an army staff car were raising a cloud of dust. As the vehicle approached, he pointed his rifle in the direction of the driver, forcing him to stop. He proceeded to ask him for the password of the day. The driver could not answer. The passenger, Regimental Colonel Levi S. Billingham, attempted to clear things up.

"At ease, soldier," he said to James, lifting the hat off his brow with his index finger. "I think you know who I am. I wasn't given the password for today, but I have business inside that cannot wait. You've done your job. Now step aside."

James felt the perspiration forming on the back of his neck. "I'm sorry, sir," he explained. "But I was given orders to get a password before allowing anyone in."

The colonel frowned and exhaled deliberately. "Exactly who gave you those orders, soldier?" he demanded.

When James explained that Swinton was the one responsible for the problem, the colonel lost his mind. He called for Swinton at once. James watched the scene from a comfortable distance.

"Captain Swinton, do you know who I am?"

"Sir, yes, sir!" Swinton replied.

"You do. Good." He pointed in the direction of James. "Does that soldier know who I am?"

"Ah, sir, I'm not sure I—"

"You stupid son of a bitch! Answer me! Does that soldier know who I am?"

"Sir, I believe he does, sir," Swinton answered uncomfortably.

Colonel Billingham was tapping two fingers against his cheek. "Then explain why I am sitting here, at the gate."

"Sir, McCleary was just following orders," Swinton explained. "Pardon the mix-up, sir. I assure you, it will not happen again."

"You're goddamned right it won't," Billingham thundered. "Orders are fine, Captain. But once in a while, pull your head out of your ass and think as well—be human for Christ sakes—or I'll have another goddamned shoe shiner back at headquarters."

The group for which he was responsible would be a challenge, beginning with Patrick McNulty, the company head case. The guys called him "Twitch" because of the nervous tick he got whenever the threat of danger presented itself. His fingernails were chewed well below the tips of his fingers, and he was always talking about dysentery or trench foot or some other malady that he was sure he had. One of the first things James noticed about him was the way he always carried an extra pair of socks, stuffed underneath his right arm.

"Hey, Twitch. What's with the socks?" he asked.

"Best way to make sure you always have a dry pair to put on. You should try it sometime, McCleary."

McNulty had difficulty with most of the other guys, especially

Tim Pearson. They were always at each other. Pearson was the kind of guy who just looked for someone to abuse. And Mc-Nulty was always in the way.

Pearson was tall and strong and, by all accounts, the best shot in the company. He was modestly handsome and witty when he wanted to be. But he was a little too aware of his attributes. He was always bragging about his many talents: weight lifting, piano playing, the way he could hit a baseball. There was no end to his boasting.

He was also a first-class complainer. It was during the trip over that they learned to turn a deaf ear each time he launched into a harangue about military incompetence and how much better he could do everything. Nothing was ever good enough. His boots were too tight. The food was tough and bland, and his bunk too narrow. The ship itself was either too big or too small, depending on which argument suited his rant. He even found a way to blame the army each time the sunshine gave way to cloud cover. He was, simply stated, a miserable son of a bitch who hated everything, everything, they noted, except the sound of his own voice.

Most often, James and Leo would just watch Pearson and shake their heads in disbelief. On the rare occasions when they actually talked to him, they found that everything associated with Pearson was either "the best" or "the worst" and that none of them could ever relate. He was one of those guys who always had a better story. James laughed at the way Pearson could "one up" them on any given occasion. His car was faster. His girl was prettier. The thing he called a bunion on his right foot was the biggest one the army medic had ever seen. And when the seas got rough that very first day, he vomited for an hour and a half longer than the rest of them.

Daniel Erikson, the burly all-American football star from Michigan and company clown, loved to see Pearson eat crow. He was always the first one to McNulty's defense. He also loved to play games. Football, pinochle, and marbles were his games of choice. His pack was filled with an assortment of trinkets and novelty items designed especially for those moments that presented an opportunity for play. He lugged around an extra two or three pounds in his pack. The other guys got on him from time to time when he fell behind on march or maneuvers.

"You better unload some of that shit in your pack, big boy," they teased. "It's slowing you down."

But it was the impromptu contests that he loved most. Erikson could make a game out of just about anything. If it hadn't been for Erikson, none of them would have known the exhilaration of racing cockroaches or the thrill of a game-winning hit during a championship round of chestnut baseball.

Once, during training camp, they were assigned to perform maneuvers in a cow pasture adjacent to camp. It was perfect training, Billings insisted. Splintered trees, craters, and clumps of torn-up earth all simulated battlefield conditions. The cows were a bit of a pain in the ass, but Billings swore it was the next best thing to actual combat. They had just completed a series of drills and were waiting for further instruction.

"Jesus Christ," one of the disgruntled soldiers moaned. "What the hell is taking so long? The smell is killing me."

They were all anxious.

The miserable situation soon became Erikson's stage. He walked away from the group. It didn't take him long.

Tim Pearson was the first to notice. The others caught on soon after and watched in disbelief as Erikson dropped to his knees and began to shape each pile of cow dung he came across into a round object the size of a bocce ball.

In just minutes, he collected a half dozen or so. He set them up neatly in rows and then began to roll the balls toward a tree about seventy-five feet from where he stood. One by one, he swung his arm back, howling each time one of the balls skipped over the tangle of roots and landed right beside the trunk.

A few of the others walked over for a closer look.

"Man, you are messed up! What the hell are you thinking, Danny boy?" one of them asked incredulously.

Erikson got a big smile on his face. "Who wants to roll for smokes, fellas?" he replied. "Closest one to the tree takes 'em all."

*

Not long after McNulty pulled James away from the corpse, they learned that they were going to stay in a stone castle that seemed to be plucked straight out of the annals of King Arthur. It was cold and gray, complete with moat and drawbridge. They looked up at the towers and imagined faces at the windows: a damsel in distress, calling to her knight in shining armor or a nefarious villain who had been captured and was awaiting his demise. It was surreal! They knew they weren't home anymore.

"Get comfortable, boys," John Sullivan announced. "Sergeant Sully says we're gonna be here a while."

"I don't believe it," Leo whispered to James. "Unreal."

At twenty years and six months, Sergeant John Sullivan, known affectionately as Sully, was the eldest of the group. Swinton called him an "an outpost expert," whatever that meant. James enjoyed being with Sully. Something about him made

James feel as though everything would turn out okay. Maybe it was that smile, or the constant laughing and joking.

Sully was a feel-good guy and the master of the superlative. Everything was "killer diller" or "18 karat." Even when he was later hit in the ass with some shrapnel and had to be transported to a dressing station twenty miles away, his head bouncing like a coconut in the back of a Jeep the entire way, all he could talk about when he got back were nurses and soft sheets.

Christopher Leonardo, "Leo," was James's oldest friend. They met the first day of training camp. James was cleaning the barracks. Leo was assigned to help him after an indiscretion with one of the sergeants.

"You got a girl back home, McCleary?" Leonardo asked.

"Sure," James answered. "Name's Madeline."

"What does she look like?"

"She's beautiful," he says, smiling from ear to ear. "Long brown hair, soft skin—nice tits. What about you?"

"A girl? Nope. Well, not really. Had one for a while. Things got a little messy toward the end. We sort of left off unfinished. I think it'll work out though. It's complicated."

"That's rough. You miss her, Leonardo? You miss home?"

"Leo. Everyone calls me Leo. A little, I guess. But I sure as hell won't shed any tears for Evansville, Indiana."

"Never been there."

"That's okay, pal." He laughed. "You're not missing too much."

"Yeah, Leo. But I bet it beats this place."

"Come on. It ain't so bad. Billings is a bit of a hump, and these boots are a bitch, but things are okay."

He wondered about Leo. Who didn't miss home? And his girl?

It was strange. And as far as Camp McCoy was concerned, "ain't so bad" wasn't exactly the way he felt about things. But if there was ever a doubt in James's mind about the kind of person Leo was, it was gone after the whole thing with the company runner.

They had just been pulled off the line to regroup. They were living in French houses that, even without heat, electricity or water, were a welcome change from the foxholes and shell holes they had begun to call home.

James and a few of the boys played cards, smoked cigars, shot craps, and wrote letters home. It was comfortable. There was a distinct smell in the air, like cinnamon or pumpkin pie. A red tablecloth, curtains, and a few soft watercolor paintings hanging just beyond the table where they sat were all soothing touches. It was almost like home.

One night, a very young soldier, younger than James, showed up at one of the card games. His name was Michael. He was the company runner. When Captain Swinton needed to contact the company sergeant, Michael was the one who delivered the message. That was his job.

Michael approached Sully with an order from Swinton: Prepare to fall out on a moment's notice.

"What do you mean fall out?" Tim Pearson bawled, frowning at the cards in his hand.

"Listen, Michele," he continued in a sultry voice, mocking the young soldier. "McNulty here still owes me six cigarettes. And I'm not going anywhere until everything is square. Now be a sweetheart and go tell Swinton he's gonna have to wait." Pearson blew him a kiss as he continued on his way. Most of the others laughed.

The runner, Michael, was small in stature. He had smooth,

soft skin and the face of a young altar boy. His features were small and effeminate. His voice was soft as well, and when he walked, everyone noticed the unusual gait created by the swaying of his hips. More than once his presence elicited derisive whistles and cat calls from Tim Pearson and some of the other guys. James watched, sometimes laughed, but never said anything.

The night that Sully's men were directed to fall out, the Germans were on the attack. By daybreak, the entire company was on the road to check them. They hooked up with a battalion of five hundred men, reinforced by air power and several tanks. James's squad was in front.

"Why is our group at the point again?" cried Pearson. He had made it very clear recently that he wanted nothing more to do with the lousy war. He had become what Leo called a "sad sack."

"I tell you what," he said to the others. "I'll walk with the rest of you suckers, but there is no way in hell I am volunteering as point man again. I nearly shit my pants the last time."

No one wanted to walk point, and they couldn't advance until someone volunteered. Everyone just stood around, waiting for someone in command to jolt them into action.

"Well, isn't this just dandy," Pearson groaned. "You know what I think? I believe that—" But before Pearson had time to utter another complaint, they were moving out. "Holy Christ," he screamed. "Someone volunteered for point man? Jesus! Who the hell is stupid enough to do that? Dumb bastard."

They followed Pearson through the group to get a look at who was leading them into battle. Ahead of the squad, maybe one hundred yards or so, was the point man: the first one to spot the enemy, the one who alerted the others, usually the first one shot, killed, or captured.

After watching their backs for a few minutes, they moved close enough to determine who it was. They could not make out his face. But the walk was unmistakable. It was Michael, company runner, leading the entire battalion of men, planes, and tanks! James and Leo could not help but smile, especially when they saw the expression on Pearson's face. It was priceless.

Leo couldn't help himself. He walked up to Pearson and pressed his lips to his ear. "What do you think of your sweetheart now, Pearson?" he whispered. "Seems to me Michele walks so funny because he's carrying your balls in his back pocket."

The only other member of the company more obnoxious than Pearson was Carmine Azzaro, the company ballbuster. Azzaro loved to stir the pot. He was a caricature of sorts: short legs, big nose, and two bushy eyebrows. He reminded James of the pictures he had seen of organ-grinders. Whenever James saw him, he always heard the hand-cranked sound of bells, whistles, and percussion and was tempted to look behind him for the tiny monkey with a little cup, dancing for his dinner. James could never understand how a guy with so many oddities could be so critical of everyone else. He was beaten up by his own men several times, all for mouthing off. Neil Hinson took him down three or four times himself.

Neil Hinson was the biggest man in the group. He was built like a farm boy: wavy blond hair, broad shoulders, and hands that looked like two baseball gloves. One of the first things that James noticed about Hinson was that nothing bothered him. There was the time Sergeant Billings made him perform an entire afternoon of military exercises in his bare feet because Hinson's boots did not meet inspection standards that morning, and Billings would have none of that. Calisthenics, sprints across a field covered with splintered stones as sharp as razors, the infamous "Billings crawl" under barbed-wire obstacles—he just kept riding him. He was merciless. But Hinson was a rock. His feet were blistered and cut. James could see the dark outline of blood snaking its way through the mud caked between his toes and around his lower ankles. It was unbelievable. The harder Billings pushed him, the more inexorable his resolve became. "What's next, sir?" he asked deadpan each time he completed the task at hand. Hinson was one tough son of a bitch. Everyone knew to steer clear, with the exception of Azzaro; he just couldn't help himself.

They were led over a dry moat filled with cracked dirt and weeds. James could feel the earth breaking beneath his boots. The air inside the castle was stale and damp; it reminded him of the way the storeroom at the Rockaway A & P smelled after a delivery had sat in crates for too long.

Once inside, James and the others were issued additional gear and equipment and were given instructions for the next two days.

It became tiring after a while for many of them, especially those who just wanted to get their first real war experience under their belts. They were scared shit, sure, but the mindless hours of waiting were interminable, far worse than anything they could imagine.

"Some of you boys said earlier that you wanted action?" Captain Swinton said. "Well, get ready. You're gonna get your wish."

Swinton selected a small group of men, headed by John Sullivan, to set up an outpost in the not too distant town of Lessay. The Germans were close. Then he told the rest of them to hunker down in the castle and follow the rules.

James and Leo were off to Lessay.

"Let's explore a little, Jimmy, before we move out," Leo said, noting the iron bars on the windows. "I can't wait to see what's downstairs."

James had other ideas. "You go ahead, Leo," he told him. "I just want to scribble a quick note to Maddie. I promised her I'd write as soon as I had the chance. I'll catch up with you later." This was the perfect time. His head was clear, and the sterile atmosphere of the cold, damp chamber provided the perfect ambience and opportunity.

THREE

✦

John sits upstairs, remembering things. So many arguments. So many things that were wrong, just plain wrong. Among the ghosts in the attic is a picture of his grandmother. Now he remembers the morning of her funeral.

"Dad," he said tearfully. "I miss Grandma. I miss her."

James had just returned home from work. He lit a cigarette and was sitting in the kitchen, wrestling with the knot of his tie while skimming through the pile of mail strewn across the table. He had that rough-day-at-work look on his face.

"Death, Jonathan, is part of life. It hurts, but you will get over it. We all do."

His mother was there to receive his frustration. She tried to help, but offered little in the way of comfort. For years she defended James and admonished *him*, insisting there were things that he just did not understand about his father.

"How many times do I have to tell you, Jonathan," she said. "Your father loves you. He does. It's just not that simple."

"What is the matter with him, Mom?" he asked. "Why does he act this way?"

"Look, Jonathan, there are things about your father you'll never know," she told him. "Things that none of us could ever understand. So don't ask, okay?"

"Why do you always say that?" he exploded. "What does that mean?"

"I don't expect you to understand, sweetheart," she said. "Just try. That's all. What do you say?"

"I hate him, Mom," he said, beginning to cry. "I hate him."

"Don't you ever say that again, young man," she warned him. "You hear me? No matter what you think or what has happened, Jonathan McCleary, he is still your father." Her breathing turned quiet. She was still, her eyes resting on her son's scowl. "Your daddy fought in the war—you just remember that. He didn't have to and he did."

John continued to press. She was on the verge of tears herself, but he could not stop. He was nine years old and beginning to resent the evasive responses to his questions. "I know about Daddy and the war," he said. "So he fought in the war. Big deal. He never talks about it. What's the big deal? Lots of other guys did."

"Just because he never said anything, dear, doesn't mean nothing ever happened."

John puts down the picture and pulls a letter from the pile. It is thicker than the others, two pages. It is folded together in the same envelope, despite the different dates written at the top of each page. He reads it and is moved by the sincerity of the words.

7 July 1944

My dearest Maddie,

Hope my letter finds you well. Where do I begin?

We landed in France with a cover of cold rain and fog along the coast. The squeaking of the seagulls stirred old, familiar feelings, like I was back with you holding hands on the beach in Rockaway. Truly a cruel trick! I miss you sweetheart.

Things here are okay, I guess. I am sorry to say that one of the first things I saw when I got here was one of our guys, dead on the side of the road. I still have not been able to get the picture out of my head. I am told I will get used to it. I sure hope not.

Don't worry darling. Things did get better. About an hour or so after our arrival, we made our way inland. I was unimpressed with the scenery. It all looked exactly like every other place I've seen. Until, of course, we came upon these hedgerows and a stone castle that looked like it was pulled off a page from a fairy tale. It is from one of these cold, empty rooms that I write this.

We will be staying here for a couple of days. We received new equipment and were given a hot meal. Not much to speak of. The day after tomorrow I will be heading out into the town of Lessay to set up an outpost.

The French peasants all smile at us and continue to celebrate our arrival with flowers, fruits, and vegetables while singing to us "Vive les Américains." Their appreciation is very touching. Most of the guys I'm with are terrific. Chris Leonardo—"Leo"— has become a real friend. He is really a swell fella. He has already

helped me immeasurably. I wish you could meet him. Right now
I am going to join him and some of the others for a little cama-
raderie before we have to move out. I'll finish writing when I get
to Lessay. To be continued . . .
    P.S. Hard to keep dry. Send socks!

He folds the first page and puts it back in the envelope. He is
intrigued by the curious postscript. He is remembering a camp-
ing trip to Schroon Lake when he was ten. He and his brothers
had wandered off in the woods, looking for frogs. When their
search proved futile, they looked elsewhere for amusement. An
old sycamore log stretched across a stream was a perfect diversion.

They climbed across the slippery log several times, pretend-
ing to be high-wire walkers, performing their death-defying act
before mesmerized spectators.

"Ladies and gentlemen, boys and girls!" they screamed, arms
outstretched, feet treading ever so carefully across the knots in
the wood. "Watch in disbelief as the amazing McCleary brothers
attempt something that has never been done before."

They crossed the stream successfully over and over, cheering
for themselves every time their sneakers landed safely on the
other side. This became easy and boring all too fast and kindled
thoughts that perhaps they should make things a little more interesting.

"Hey, Johnny," Paul said. "How about we run across this time
instead of walking?"

John smiled. "Ladies and gentlemen!" he screamed again.
"Just when you thought you had seen it all . . ."

Off they went, daring and reckless, running, skipping, and
jumping across the fallen sycamore. They were singing and

laughing and bragging about how amazing they were. Until they pushed it too far.

It wasn't long before one of them fell victim to the moss that covered the top side of the log. In John went. He was soaked up to his knees. Uncomfortable with the way his wet socks felt in his sneakers, he took them off and prepared his best Whitey Ford impersonation.

"Matty, watch this!" he said, before rolling them up in a ball and hurling them into the stream.

When he arrived back at their cabin, James was sitting quietly on the porch with Madeline. They both watched hypnotically as a pair of cardinals darted back and forth between a perch high atop a Scotch pine and a Victorian birdfeeder brimming with raisins and sunflower seeds.

"We should get away more often, James," Madeline said to him. He leaned closer to her and grabbed her hand.

"It is nice," he said. "Quiet."

"There's no reason why we can't," she continued. "The pharmacy runs okay when you are not there. Look, here come the boys."

John and his brothers came bounding out of the woods, laughing and carrying on. One look at John's feet, and James was in orbit.

"Where the hell are your socks, Jonathan!" he thundered.

"They got wet," he said. "So I threw them out."

"You did what!"

Madeline looked at James and ran her hand gently over his back.

"I threw them out," John explained. "I have another pair inside."

"I don't care how many goddamned pairs you have," James screamed. "You march your ass back into those woods and get those socks!"

John trudged off back to the stream. He hated his father.

"They're just socks," he mumbled under his breath. "What's the big deal?"

FOUR

★

The Norman hedgerows were a nightmare. Like most of the American soldiers, James and his company were ill equipped to negotiate the labyrinthine rows of enclosed fields and sunken lanes. They had never seen anything like it. Sully said it reminded him of the caves at Howe Caverns he visited with his family one summer when he was a kid.

"It had a flat ceiling, and the walls were close, just like these," he explained. "You really couldn't see a goddamned thing. It was kind of cool."

Azzaro's opinion was a lot more critical: "How the hell are we supposed to fight a goddamned war in this shit?" he bawled.

The trepidation would only get worse. On one of the first

scouting patrols, they found a German soldier lying in a ravine. His ankle had been torn off by a mortar. He was crying and begging for someone to help him.

"*Hilferufe! Ami. Hilferufe!*" he cried when he saw them coming. They all looked at the dying man with confusion.

"What should we do, Sully?" James asked.

Sully tipped his helmet up with the barrel of his rifle and shook his head. He was about to say something when Neil Hinson walked over to the writhing German and put a pistol in between his eyes and pulled the trigger. Blood shot out all over the front of Hinson's uniform. He didn't even blink. Just took out a handkerchief and wiped his face. Then he spent the next few minutes showing everyone the machine pistol he lifted from the dead man's body.

Azzaro looked on with eyes both wide and wet with fear. "That is fucked up," he whispered under his breath. James just watched.

The thick vegetation, comprised of dense hedges and small trees set at odd angles, grew in an earthen embankment three to five feet tall and at times just as thick. Visibility was poor. They were squeezed in on both sides by massive walls of vegetation. One step inside, and their tie to the outside world was severed. They wandered in circles. Some got lost; they had nothing to guide them. Even the sky was taken away; the branches on either side of the road they traveled embraced at the top, forming a leafy canopy that suffocated the air and light. They went on ceaselessly. All they had was each other.

"Hey, Sully," Leo called from behind. "Twitch and I want to know what you did back in New Jersey. You know, for a living."

Sully turned around and smiled. "I have two cigarettes in my pocket for the guy who guesses right," he answered.

James laughed, then ran up ahead to walk with Sully at the front of the line. "What's up, McCleary? You want a piece of the action also?"

"No, no. I was just wondering what we can expect, Sully. I mean, it's so damn quiet."

"Don't know, McCleary," Sully said. "That's the beauty of the hedgerow. You just never know."

James listened to the sound of their boots on the loose ground. It was grating, like wet clothes being dragged across a washboard. He wondered if it bothered the others. And if the Germans could hear. It felt odd too. The earth was soft and granular, almost like the sand bars in Rockaway he climbed on as a kid.

"So you're from Jersey," James said.

"Yup. Plainfield, a little town just south of Linden. What about you, McCleary?"

"Rockaway Beach," he said. "New York."

Sully's eyes lit up. "Rockaway Beach?" he repeated. "Did you ever go to that dance hall—now what the hell was the name of it?"

"Spinning Wheel."

"Yeah, that's it!" Sully said. "You know it?"

"Sure," James said. "It's not too far from my house."

"Man, I had some really killer-diller times there. That place, and Billie's. You know Billie's?"

James smiled.

"My cousin and I would sneak out at night sometimes when we were visiting my aunt in Roxbury," Sully explained. "Damn, those were good times."

They talked about Rockaway Beach and all the places they both had been. It felt good to have familiar names on his lips:

the Park Theater, the boardwalk, Billie's Tavern. God, he missed home. They continued their game of "what about this place" until some of the other guys in back started to ride James.

"Hey, McCleary," Leo yelled. "Can someone else have a turn with Sully? People are starting to talk. And Twitch over here is getting a little jealous. Besides, we need you to settle an argument back here."

James fell back with the others. Azzaro and Hinson were embroiled in a heated debate. Hinson towered over Azzaro and could crush him like a bug with little effort. Still, Azzaro couldn't help himself.

"What are you two idiots arguing about now?" James asked.

"McCleary," Azzaro began, getting right up in James's face. "Now listen to me. You're an athletic guy. Would you please tell this country bumpkin that riding horses is not a sport."

"Oh, you have got to be kidding me, Azzaro," James said. "That's what you're fighting about?"

Hinson was shaking his head. "It's not me, McCleary. I want nothing to do with that little shit. All I was doing was telling Leonardo about my farm back home and how rough it is to ride some of those horses. Then Azzaro started spouting off again."

"It's not a sport, hayseed!" Azzaro screamed, listening to Hinson and James. "Is there a ball? A winner and loser? Jesus! Just admit I'm right!"

"I'm warning you, Azzaro, you little bastard. Get away from me. Now!"

"Why do you care so much anyway, Azzaro?" Pearson asked. "It's not like you're ever gonna ride one through the streets of Brooklyn."

That caught Hinson's attention. "I don't know about that," he called back. "Have you seen that picture of his girl?"

James pulled Hinson away from Azzaro before there was another incident. As they talked, they could hear Azzaro's voice in the distance, pleading his case to the others.

"So, do you have many guys like him in Kansas?" James said laughing.

"We had one," Hinson recalled. "Roy Gainey. A little guy, just like Azzaro. Hung him up by his underpants, right from the crane hook outside the barn."

James laughed. "What did you do with him?" he asked.

"Nothing," Hinson explained. "Just left him there for two hours or so. We didn't ignore him though. A few eggs and some rotten tomatoes found their way up to him."

The strap on James's helmet was digging into his chin. He tried to adjust it without his hands, moving his head back and forth. Finally, he put his gun under his arm and undid the clasp, letting the strap fall to the side of his face.

"What's it like growing up on a farm?" James asked.

"It's good, I guess," Hinson said. "Don't know any other way."

"Any brothers or sisters at home?"

"Two sisters and two brothers," Hinson told him. "I'm the second in order. My older brother is Navy."

"Just the five of you," James teased. "I thought farm families were huge?"

"Well, my mama wanted to have more. Just didn't work out. Like she always says, 'Men make plans and God laughs.'"

James smiled. It was the sort of thing his own mother would say.

"What about you, McCleary? Brothers and sisters?"

"Two brothers," James said. "Both younger."

"You guys close?" Hinson asked.

"Yeah, I guess so. I mean, my dad died when I was nine, so I sort of became the one they looked to. Mom was always busy, working."

They moved down the hedgerow, twisting and turning as they slipped deeper and deeper into the maze of vegetation. They were disoriented. They all knew it, but no one wanted to utter the horrible words. On one side of their row was an open area, a field of some sort; they caught a glimpse every now and again through the intermittent breaks in the thickets. On the other side was another row, just like the one they were navigating. Everything looked the same. They walked for quite some time, hoping for a way out. Eventually, they came to a spot where the brush was noticeably thinner.

"Sully," the others called to him. "Hold up a minute."

Sully turned around to see Twitch, Erikson, and Azzaro with their pants open, relieving themselves on one of the trees. "Well, isn't this a sight?" he laughed.

Sully and some of the others talked while waiting for the three of them to zip up. "How much farther till we see a break," James asked.

"Not sure, McCleary. No real way to tell. Hopefully, we'll be in Lessay by nightfall."

"Do you expect German activity?" Leo asked.

Sully shrugged his shoulders. He was growing impatient standing there. "Hey, hurry up back there," he screamed to the peeing trio.

"Coming, Sarge," Erikson called back. "I'm just signing my name."

They were off again, the hope of finding a way out drawing
them on. It had begun to drizzle, a cold, steady sprinkle that
seemed to hang in the air just long enough to find its way underneath their clothing. James had walked the last mile or so
with Leo in virtual silence; his thoughts had drifted back to
Madeline and Rockaway. The monotony of patrolling the
hedgerows for hours had enervated his resolve, and his mind
wandered.

And then it all changed. James was back in the war. They
stopped suddenly and drew their guns, pointing them in the direction of a peculiar rustling coming from the other side of the
bushes. Sully motioned to hold all fire. They stood still and listened intently.

James's eyes darted back and forth between the tangled
brush and the faces of his comrades. Their expressions were as
varied as their personalities. Sully was cool; Erikson postured
with anticipation; Leo's smile melted into a scowl; and Hinson,
Pearson, and Azzaro all had one eye closed and the other focused on a point somewhere in the thickets. All was still except
for some dry leaves dancing in the faint breeze and the spasmodic movement of Patrick McNulty's lip.

The rustling grew more distinct. And closer. It sounded like
arms and legs struggling against the uncompromising tangle of
branches and twigs. Sully's hand remained in the air. The others held their positions. And watched. They were worried but in
control. All except McNulty, who was crumbling.

The twitching became more pronounced. Tears filled his
eyes. James thought he heard him say something seconds before he opened fire, emptying his weapon into the clump of
hedges.

The stillness following McNulty's outburst was broken by a thump behind the thicket.

"Fix bayonets," Sully ordered. The sound of clicking echoed ominously. Then he moved forward and parted the branches in front of him to take a look, thoughts centering on the enemy and face-to-face combat. His head wasn't more than halfway through the opening when he exhaled heavily and smiled.

"Oh, holy shit!" he said, laughing uncontrollably.

"What the hell is so funny?" McNulty asked.

"Go on," Sully told them, grabbing his sides. "See for yourselves."

There, lying in front of them, was a wayward cow who had been grazing on the tall wisps of grass along the side of the row.

"Nice going, Twitch," Azzaro teased. "You killed a fucking cow."

"Drop dead, Azzaro," he answered. "How the hell was I supposed to know? You all thought it was a kraut too!"

Hinson, who was the only one who had not laughed at the absurd reality, spoke gravely. "You shouldn't have fired your weapon," he said.

"What?" McNulty questioned.

"You shouldn't have fired your weapon."

"What the hell is that supposed to mean?" McNulty complained. "Big deal," he continued to protest. "It's a goddamned cow."

Hinson pushed past McNulty and the others. The cow just lay there, eyes dark and round, groaning, until Hinson, quietly and apparently with no emotion, buried a bullet in the back of its head.

FIVE

*

It is morning. John begins his day by pulling the second part of the letter from the envelope. It was written, he sees, eight days later. He looks at his watch and then back at the piles of junk that need to be sorted. He puts the letter back for a minute, then pulls it out again. There is still much to be done, but it is early.

He reads. The tone is much different, somber and melancholy. Halfway down the page, he stops again. He is sure he has heard something, like footsteps on the stairs. He pushes the letter into his pocket and creeps down the staircase to investigate. Through the painted spindles, John sees James, still at the window, legs crossed, arms folded. He sits down on one of the steps, his chin resting comfortably in his palms, and looks at this old, scrawny man he scarcely knows.

The sun has inched over the peaks of the houses across the street, casting peculiar shadows all across the room. The disappointment of years past lurks in those shadows. Will it always be there, he wonders, this dark place struggling in the light of the present?

In the early-morning light, James looks old, much older than he ever has. Strange. John feels the same, as if he hasn't aged at all. He could wake up tomorrow and learn that he has an algebra test fourth period, and wouldn't think twice about it. In many ways, he is still the same awkward kid, wading through the murky, tumultuous tide of adolescence. The shot of his father is an incongruous reality. His face is weathered. He is completely bald with the exception of a few stray wisps of silver. The strong hands are now wrinkled and dry, like a beaten up pair of old leather shoes. The voice is weak and tremulous.

Madeline's death has all but destroyed him. John thinks of her, lying in St. Charles Cemetery, beneath the freshly turned earth and rocks. He wonders if the grass has started to grow. And if the headstone has been set. He wishes he could talk to her, just for a minute, just to say good-bye.

Outside, the wind is blowing and smacks the warped gray shutters hard against the shingles. The sound jars him from his thoughts. He looks at the old man again, wonders what he is thinking and how he will make it without her. The wind howls. A draft slips into the room and tickles the gauzy curtains that hang beside his father's chair. James shudders.

Satisfied that his father is resigned to just sit by himself,

John returns to the attic and begins reading the letter again from the top.

15 July 1944

I am back. Sorry it took so long. A lot has happened. Eight days have passed. It's hard to believe. How I long to hold you close again. I think of you often each day and dream about you at night. I am okay.

Things here are not exactly what I expected. We had some losses recently. It has been really hard to accept. I am unharmed, but I really don't sleep anymore. My mind feels so full. I wish I could tell you more.

It is far more difficult than I ever could have imagined. I am making it; how I don't know. I really do not understand this war. There is so much I want to tell you but can't. Even if I could, where to begin I would not know.

I miss you and everyone back home. I will write again soon when I get the chance. Until then, you are in my thoughts and prayers. Send my love to my mom and the boys.

Forever yours,

Jimmy

There are many things the letter does not say, things that John will never know. Like the phrase "establish position." It was such a curious expression. James hated when Swinton said it. Did anyone ever really establish position? And what did that mean anyway?

After killing the cow, they wandered into the abandoned town of Lessay shortly after dawn. They unloaded their gear and set up in a defunct warehouse just outside the village. Only three of them had been in this situation before.

Sully was cool and put them all at ease. James liked him from the minute he met him. He was the first person he met, with the exception of Leo, who reminded him of home.

"Okay, boys," he bellowed, clearing a space for his pack and blanket. "Let the good times roll."

For Sully, life at an outpost was terrific. "There's something about an outpost, fellas!" he said smiling. He treated these opportunities like it was some kind of poker game but without the chips, the alcohol, and the music. Nothing else in wartime let the soldier sit for such extended periods of time and shoot the bull.

It was during these times that strangers became brothers. They shared everything. How else would anyone have known that Carmine Azzaro became a man with Maryanne Lupoli in the backseat of his father's Ford? Or that the half-moon–shaped scar two inches above Neil Hinson's right eye was from an errant kick by a cow he was milking while working his grandfather's farm in Kansas? After a few days at an outpost, there were no more secrets. Killer-diller.

They talked about everything: girls, cars, baseball, and, of course, food. It was the one thing they never stopped thinking about.

To pass the nights, they vividly described dishes they all fantasized about: ginger-broiled chicken, beef tenderloin steak with mushrooms and glazed onions, crown roast of pork with apple stuffing and cider gravy. Each one of them took great pride in his selection. The objective was simple: to create the biggest commotion among those who were starving.

Carmine Azzaro was the best at it. He called it mouthwater torture and had perfected the art. He never missed an opportunity to break balls.

"Okay, fellas. Who wants to hear my menu for tonight?" he said, leaning his head against his duffle bag.

"Enough with it, Azzaro, you stupid dago," Hinson screamed. "No one's in the mood tonight."

"What's the matter, Hinson? The chipped beef ain't sitting well with you this evening?"

Neil Hinson was not only the biggest in the group but also the biggest eater and the one who had the least tolerance for Azzaro's bullshit. He had warned him several times before to steer clear, but Azzaro didn't listen.

"Come on, Carmine," James said. "It's been a long day. Lay off."

"Relax, ladies. I'm just trying to lighten the mood a little. So we won't talk about dinner tonight."

"Cool," Sully added. "We'll try something else. Anyone have any suggestions?"

"Well, let's see," James said. "We've covered girlfriends, cars, sports, and mothers. What the hell is left?"

"I got one, McCleary," Azzaro said. "How about desserts?"

Hinson got to his feet and rolled up his sleeve. "I'm telling you right now, Azzaro, you little shit," Hinson warned. "One more word about food, and I'll rip your head off."

"You know what, guys, on second thought, it might be best if we hit the hay early tonight," Sully suggested.

There was a little grumbling, but soon it was quiet. Each man lay still, lost in distant thoughts.

The minutes passed. Now the only audible sounds were

singing crickets and the distant drone of falling shells. They had forgotten about their hunger and were all just about asleep when a raspy voice with a heavy Brooklyn accent broke the silence. "Warm apple pie with vanilla ice cream."

Hinson pounced on Azzaro, smashing Carmine's nose with his fist. It took three of them to pull him off.

*

Six days passed. The waiting was killing all of them. It was bad enough they had to fight these goddamned krauts—it was the last thing any of them wanted to do—but to wait there for them on the chance they *might* be coming?

Each of them grabbed a wooden box, dragged it across the concrete floor and rested. The cold, dark metal beams that stretched across the ceiling looked like railroad tracks. James leaned his head back and smiled, imagining for a moment the train he occasionally rode to New York City.

The moonlight struggled to penetrate the windows that were clouded with soot until the butt end of Leo's rifle released a flood of warm beams into the room. With proper ventilation, Azzaro suggested they make a fire. But Sully insisted that the Germans would spot them instantly. So they abandoned the idea and sat together, in a horseshoe, tired and frustrated.

"Hey, Sully," Azzaro finally asked. "When are we going to call it quits? The krauts aren't coming. How about giving Swinton a call?"

The days had become long and tiresome. The offensive was obviously not coming. They were ready to go back.

"Come on, Carmine," Sully shot back. "These are United States Army, first-class, killer-diller accommodations." His

breath smelled of tobacco. "Where else are you gonna score sil-
verware and a mattress?"

"Azzaro's got a point, Sully," Hinson said. "You're happy to
sit around and smoke. But the rest of us want out. Christ, we
haven't seen anything in days."

"Yeah," added James. "What do you say, Sully? How about
giving Swinton a ring?"

John Sullivan was not one for quitting. And putting a premature end to the party was not something he wanted to do. Still,
he agreed to make the call.

Sully was told to send five of his men back to the command
post. They drew straws, and Walker, Tucker, Alberts, Burkhart,
and Leonardo were the big winners. The others would join the
rest of the company the next morning.

The lucky five were filling up their packs and gathering the
rest of their belongings when the whistling of falling shells, followed by a thump, something like a door falling, interrupted
the peace. Then the sound of feet displacing piles of rubble
grew louder and louder. Everyone ran for cover, ducking behind crates or lying behind toppled piles of rocks.

"In coming!" they all screamed, scrambling to all corners of
the warehouse.

James was frozen. He couldn't move. All he could do was listen to Sully's voice, coming from behind a shattered stone wall.
He was talking frantically to Swinton. His voice was tremulous.

It was hard to believe, but it was true: the Germans had them
surrounded. James heard them talking. He knew he had to find
cover, but before he could move, a shrill groan pierced the air
and a metal beam from the railroad ceiling came crashing

down, pinning him between a radiator and the dusty concrete floor.

"We're under attack!" Sully cried into the receiver. "Captain, we are in need of reinforcements. The . . . the Germans . . . they're in the next room." James just listened.

Sully's voice grew more urgent with each second. "What the hell do you mean 'do the best we can'? Captain, we are in need of assistance. Captain! Captain!"

There was silence on the other end. Swinton didn't want to risk losing the whole group. What would the general think?

"Goddammit!" Sully bawled, firing the phone into the pile of debris. They were on their own.

The German soldiers poured into the warehouse, the smoky air punctured by the report of gunfire. James saw everything. The Germans passed right over him. Sully was the first to fall. Hinson was next. James watched in horror from beneath the beam.

Carmine and the others emerged with their hands feebly in the air. James wanted to stand up, to take his rightful position next to his brothers, but he couldn't. He remained silent, his body wedged between fragments of wood and iron.

His cheek rested against a cool pipe. The sensation bothered him, but he could not move. He struggled for every breath, the hands of the beam tightening their grasp with every minute that passed. He watched as the Germans stripped the others of their weapons and pushed them toward the door. They were smiling. Their uniforms were clean. He closed his eyes. James was praying for his comrades. He was praying that the Germans would not find him. Above all else, he was praying to Sully and Hinson for forgiveness.

He remained pinned against the radiator. He thought of Madeline and his mother, how they would react when they heard the news. With his eyes closed, he could picture the candles on the altar at St. Rose of Lima Church and hear Father Lanning's voice, cold and vituperative. "What will you say, James McCleary, when you meet Jesus?"

He always found that question to be comical in a most absurd way. How do you answer such a question? Would Jesus even want to talk to him? Lying there, he thought about it again and still had no idea. What would he say? The truth was, he had never really thought about it at all. Not really. More than anything, he had always thought he would have time to figure it out, that the day of reckoning would come much later on, when he was wrinkled and gray and had time enough to formulate an appropriate response. He was unprepared; he began to pray anyway, hoping Jesus would somehow understand.

And then, as quickly as it had begun, it was over. The gunfire ceased, leaving nothing but the sound of men clinging to their very last breath. That, too, faded, and all James could hear was the sound of boots on gravel, dying in the distance.

The meeting would have to wait. A unit from another division came through an hour later and pulled James from the pile. At first, he thought he was dreaming. The faces of the two soldiers who freed his legs looked like reflections cast in swirling water. Before long, the haze lifted, and he was returned to his company.

The first face he saw when he got back was Leo's.

"McCleary? Holy shit!" he screamed in celebration. "What the hell happened?"

"The krauts. They were everywhere. I thought I was done."

Leo's face grew somber. "Sully? Hinson?" he asked.

"Yup. They never had a chance. That son of a bitch Swinton sold us out. I heard the whole thing."

The two continued to talk until Swinton's arrival interrupted their reunion.

"McCleary? Is that you?" he asked incredulously.

"Yeah, it's me, you motherfucker! 'Establish position. Scout for Germans. Do the best you can.' Yeah. That one's a beauty. 'Do the best you can.' That's definitely my favorite."

"Fall back, McCleary. You don't know what you're talking about."

"Didn't think anyone would ever know about it, did ya?" James continued viciously. "What kind of a lily-livered chicken-shit are you? Do the best you can? You hung us out to dry, you son of a bitch."

"Are you kidding me, McCleary!" Swinton roared. "You want to take me on?"

James spit at Swinton's feet. "I wouldn't piss on you if you were on fire," he said.

Swinton rushed for James. Leo stepped in the way and separated the two of them.

Swinton got over it and continued to lead the group—he had responsibilities—but James never forgot.

SIX

✪

John separates the dusty contents of the attic into two piles: garbage and that which will be boxed and moved to one of their houses.

His hands brush away a gauzy veil of cobweb. Behind most of the free-standing objects sit large cardboard boxes overstuffed with novelty items and memorabilia.

Much of what he moves is heavy. He tries to dislodge a small aluminum canoe that is stretched across still more boxes. It teeters precariously on two cardboard arches formed by cartons stacked carelessly underneath. He recognizes a swatch of green canvas wedged in between two wooden crates below. He moves closer and bends down for a closer look. The canoe blocks his path. He drops to his knees. He strains to slide one of the crates off to the side; it will not budge. He tries the other. Nothing doing. Frustrated, he leans in even closer, turns his head sideways, and reaches in between as far as he can, groping for the thin line of frayed rope that hangs off one of the ends of the canvas. After several tries, his fingers finally find the braided cord. He pulls hard and manages to loosen the canvas but jerks his hand away violently after puncturing his index finger on a metal hook he failed to see.

"Goddammit!" he screams, pressing the area with his thumb to test the severity of the injury. A perfect bead of red rises to the surface. He is just about to go downstairs for a Band-Aid when his phones rings. It is his brother Matt.

"Johnny, is the realtor coming by today?" he asks.

"I'm not sure," John answers, putting his finger in his mouth. "I told her I'd be here all week."

"You sound funny," Matt says. "Is everything okay?"

"Yeah, everything's fine," John says. "I just cut my fucking finger trying to move something. Remember dad's hammock?"

"No way!" Matt screams. "That old, green piece of shit?" He is laughing at John.

"Yup. I caught myself on one of the hooks." John cleans the bloody finger with his mouth, then wipes it dry on his jeans.

"What are you going to do with it?" Matt asks.

"Are you kidding me?" John barks. "It's going out with the rest of the shit up here."

"Dad doesn't want it?"

"Trust me, Matt," John explains. "He won't miss it." John continues to slide the hammock away from the boxes while he talks.

"Boy, things sure have changed, huh?" Matt muses. "There was a time when he never would have parted with that thing. Remember? Every trip we took, he had to bring that stupid thing."

Matt moves the conversation to his own vacation plans. His voice trails off. John's mind drifts as memories begin to invade his thoughts. He is remembering an exchange between him and his father. It was a hot, sticky day. The mosquitoes drifting lazily around the periphery of the lake were biting, sending all of them back to the cabin for the afternoon. Madeline and the boys were inside. James was in the back, his eyes closed and body suspended in the folds of a hammock stretched between two giant evergreens. The smell of pine needles, cigarette smoke, and Old Spice aftershave was strong in the air.

John slipped out the back and approached James, who continued to lie motionless, hands folded on his chest, a pale blue fishing hat pulled snugly over his brow.

"Daddy, will you show me how to put a worm on a hook?" John asked.

"Not now, Jonathan," James told him. "Later. The fish are not biting."

He kicked the dirt. "Well, I'm bored," he protested. "Can we go for a hike or something? I found a really cool trail. I can show you, just over the hill."

James continued to speak to John from underneath his hat. "We have two more days to do that," he said. "Why don't you see what your mom is up to."

John frowned. He extended his foot back and sent a pine-cone skipping across the grass. As he turned to go inside, his father spoke.

"Before you go, Johnny, would you hand me my beer?"

John bent down and grabbed the bottle, but the condensation on it made it slip through his hand. The glass shattered against a rock.

"What the hell is wrong with you, Jonathan!" James exploded. "Jesus Christ! All I ask for is a little relaxation, some peace and quiet. Is that too much to ask?"

★

John recalls the tears and the argument he heard from behind the cabin door:

"What in God's name is going on with you, James McCleary?" Madeline said. "It was just an accident."

"Well, that doesn't really change anything, now does it!" James snapped back.

"He just wants to be with you," she tried to explain. "That's all. Can't you see that?"

"I came up here to relax, Madeline, goddammit! Not to play babysitter every time one of the kids asks for something. I've had it! Enough of this! Get the suitcases ready. We're leaving!"

"Leaving? We just—"

"I said we're leaving!" he screamed. "This was a big mistake!"

Less than two hours later, the car was on the road, rolling quietly back to Rockaway. All because he spilled a goddamned beer.

★

When he hangs up the phone, he decides to give his finger more serious attention. "Hey, Pop. Do we have any Band-Aids lying around?" he asks.

James appears annoyed.

"I doubt it," he says. "But you can check the medical kit. Should be under the sink in the kitchen."

It doesn't take him long to find the blue and white box. All that remains in the cabinet are some old baby-food jars and an empty box of steel wool.

"Do you want me to save anything of yours from upstairs?" he asks, wrapping the plastic bandage around his finger. "I mean, before I throw it out." He is thinking of that goddamned hammock.

"No," James replies. "It's not necessary."

"Okay," he says. "Just thought I'd ask."

*

There was a tacit understanding among his family, an unspoken acknowledgment that something was different about the man they called husband and father. This man who got out of bed every day at four-thirty in the morning, who patched and painted the plaster walls, and manicured the shrubbery meticulously, was just a shadow who wandered through the house. This man who lived among them was a stranger in so many ways.

His behavior rarely changed. John returned home from baseball practice one evening. James, as usual, was seated in his chair, smoking a cigarette, scotch in hand. The TV was dark, yet his gaze was off in that direction. John looked at his dad but said nothing. The old man hardly stirred.

"Is that you, Johnny?" Madeline called from the kitchen.

"Yeah, Mom." He dropped his books on the end table and took a couple of steps toward the other room. Whatever his mother was cooking sure smelled great.

"Take your books to your room," his father mumbled to him. He didn't even look at him. He lifted the scotch to his lips. The monotone infuriated John like nothing else.

In the beginning, when the children were small, Madeline pressed the issue with him. Each time she saw her husband struggling, she felt a pounding in her chest that ran through her body until finding its resting place in the tips of all of her extremities. Perhaps it wasn't emotional at all, not completely anyway. Maybe it was physiological. Maybe it was her body's way of saying that there were things in her home that needed to be fixed. The signs were everywhere. She saw the pained expression on her children's faces each time they extended themselves to him, only to be brushed aside in favor of a newspaper or scotch bottle. He had done the same thing to her many times before.

"Why are you so unavailable, James?" she asked on several occasions. This became the way they began and ended many of their conversations.

John was the one who had suffered the most. He was willful and precocious. He was also sensitive. There were many nights, after dinner, when young John sneaked into the living room where James sat in silence by the window and wormed his way onto his father's lap. The smell of cigarette smoke and liquor was strong. The two of them sat together in the big brown chair that Madeline had placed next to the picture window. It was enough for him just to sit and be close to his father. Sometimes an entire hour passed before they exchanged a single word. There were times when nothing was said at all. John was patient. He sat quietly for minutes at a time, looking at his father while tracing in his mind's eye the outline of his face, beginning at the cleft in his chin and ending at the tiny "v" formed by the lines on his forehead.

On the rare occasion when there was discussion, John was the one who broke the stillness.

"What are you thinking about, Daddy?" he asked. It was a question that he would repeat again and again for many years to come. But his patience diminished with time, as did his willingness to hear his mother's excuses. As a small child, John had difficulty articulating what it was, but he knew that something was wrong. It felt wrong. Now seeing his friends' fathers shed light on his own dad gave everything that was wrong with him a shape, if not a name. The indescribable void had found a voice.

John was the first of the boys to wade into the uncharted waters. It happened one night after sitting with his father in the big brown chair.

"Steven Cooper's dad plays tag with Steven and all of his brothers and sisters in their backyard," he complained to Madeline. "And hide-and-seek and cowboys-and-indians and baseball."

As she folded laundry in the bedroom, Madeline listened while her eldest child struggled through a difficult realization.

"He laughs a lot too."

"Johnny," Madeline said softly. "What's wrong, honey? What's bothering you? Do you want to ask me something?"

"I love Daddy, Mom. You know, he's my dad. But why, why doesn't he do those kinds of things with us? You know, laugh, joke around."

"Your father loves you, Jonathan. He loves all of us. Can't that be enough?"

*

Not much changed with time. In the final week of June in his freshman year of high school, John found out he had failed his algebra class and that he had to attend summer school instead of traveling to Florida with one of his friends. He sat with his mother at the kitchen table, crying his eyes out and explaining the frustration he felt with the equations.

"I just don't understand the stuff," he complained. His mother's attention was comforting.

His father entered the room, cigarette dangling from his lips, looking for a book of matches. "Fine time to be worrying about it," he commented, his back to the two of them as he rummaged through the junk drawer.

"Thank you, Dad, for understanding," he said. "Thanks for the support."

James struck a match, leaving a faint cloud of smoke behind him. He heard the rumblings. They all thought he was oblivious, but the truth was he knew very well what was being said about him in his house. He knew that the children found it difficult to be with him and that they went to Madeline for everything. Especially John. It was troubling, but not enough to change anything. He had learned that sometimes a person needs to take care of *himself*, to make sense of who he was and where he was headed. Some would call it selfishness. For James it was survival.

It kept him awake at night, staring at the twisted shadows that extended from the top of the back wall of their bedroom across and onto the ceiling. He lay still sometimes for hours, listening to his own breathing, forced and heavy, as though it was coming from someone else lying there between him and Madeline.

He felt crazy sometimes. Certifiable. As if he had somehow stepped out of his body and now, as punishment, was being forced to look at himself with the eyes of a stranger. It was maddening. All those months, crawling on his belly in the mud and snow like a stupid son of a bitch, waiting, just waiting for some trigger-happy kraut to pop him. What did it mean now, lying in the dark? Back then his rage had an outlet, a target. It felt good. Where was that target now?

Night was the time he looked for the answer. The silence helped him think. He wrestled with a series of "what-ifs" and "could-ofs" and "should-ofs," determined to find some sort of resolution. It never came.

When his eyelids finally became too weak to support the weight of this restlessness, he let them close. On most nights, this was a blessing, for his mind welcomed the respite from the echoes of the infantry, which droned on. During the hours when James slept, he was free, liberated temporarily from certain thoughts that polluted his mind. But there were many nights when the dreams came almost the second he drifted off. They were vivid and real and always the same.

The struggle with Madeline and his boys was always worse when he dreamed. He could never say the things he wanted. They were just shadows, faceless shapes that swirled in desultory circles. And, of course, images of Sully and Leo and the rest of the guys never faded. All those memories were sharp, faces that spilled into the shadows, creating a disturbing patchwork that displayed the scenes from his present and past.

He would awaken when the morning sun slipped over the peak of the neighbor's rooftop and through their window. It was morning again, and like every morning, he'd be no further along than he had been the previous day.

SEVEN

*

As promised, Matt and Paul head over to the house after work to help John. When they pull up, they both notice some old furniture and a couple of green garbage bags.

The screen door is partially open. They slip inside unnoticed. James is sitting in his chair, rocking back and forth, in front of the television.

Matt and Paul walk past unseen and climb the stairs. In the far corner of the attic, John is sitting on a crate with his back to them. He is reading. They consider, for a moment, sneaking up on him the way they used to when they were kids, but the somber mood prevails.

"Johnny," Matt calls from the stairwell. "I don't see too much stuff on the curb. What the hell have you been doing all day?"

John is startled. He slips the letter he is holding, along with the others, under an old comforter that he had placed over his father's footlocker.

"Hey, it's about time you two clowns showed up. Let's go. There's a lot of crap up here."

The three of them sit in different parts of the attic, opening boxes and sorting through items that have lain dormant for years. Everything they touch sets in motion waves of images that usher in reflections of lives that remain, in many respects, a mystery.

"I spoke to Lucy Cunningham today," John says. "The real estate agent."

"Yeah?" Matt questions.

"Says she has a buyer. A couple, relocating from Buffalo. But she wants the house empty."

"So, what does that mean?" Paul asks.

"What that means, Paul," John says, dumping a handful of old greeting cards into a cardboard box designated for trash, "is that you better start moving your ass."

"Hey, would you look at this?" Paul is holding an old photograph up to the light. "Can you believe what mom and dad looked like when they were young? God, this is creepy. I look just like him."

"While you're at it," Matt teases, "take a good look at the man downstairs as well. That's you, little Pauly, in about fifty years."

After they've had their fun needling each other, they begin hinting at all of the things about their father they resent. The undercurrent of tension, the emotional distance, the alarming stoicism, and perfunctory movements that challenge the idea that the man is actually alive.

"Remember that Christmas," John says, "when Dad got stuck playing Santa Claus at that party they used to have every year because Uncle Victor had kidney stones?"

"Yeah," Matt says, shaking his head. They are all remembering a man whose dour expression could still be seen behind eyeglasses and a beard of snowy white. Even little Caroline Buckley, who hopped up on his lap and, sweet as could be, asked him if she could have one of his reindeer, could not melt the man's heart.

"I don't think I can remember even one time when I saw him laugh," Paul recalls.

Being together is therapeutic for each of them. They spend much of the evening sifting through piles of junk and telling tales of exile and disappointment. They are orphans now. Not in the conventional manner, but the sense of abandonment is certainly there. John in particular finds comfort in hearing the other two speak of things that continue to fester in his own mind, many of which he has yet to articulate or really define.

There were so many days they can recall when James just faded into the background. He was always too busy to play games of catch or to fix a flat bicycle tire. The more they talked, the more vivid the memories became.

"How many father-son Boy Scout picnics can you actually miss before you lose the title," Matt asks.

"And Mom always protected him," John says bitterly. "No matter what."

Paul is suddenly aware of the time. He groans and throws his hands up.

"There's too much crap up here, John. We're never gonna get done. What the hell are we supposed to do with it all?"

"It's simple, Pauly. Keep what you want. Everything else gets tossed."

"Shouldn't we get Dad up here?" Matt says. "Ask him about some of this stuff? I mean, it is his house."

"He doesn't care," John says. "Told me to get rid of all of it."

"You think that's normal?" Matt adds. "There's not *one* thing up here he wants?"

"Normal?" John repeats. "Normal? Tell me Matt. Just what the hell does that mean, anyway?"

The next day, John is back at it again. It has been storming for hours. He is tired. There is still much to do. He sits quietly, smoking a cigarette while looking out the tiny window in the attic. The rain beats hard against the side of the house.

*

It was the November of his twenty-third year. At his mother's request, he flew in from California for Thanksgiving. It was the first time he had done so in years.

The cold November rain spilled over the sides of umbrellas and newspapers held high as weary travelers exited the terminals at JFK and dashed frantically for taxicabs. John was three hours late and found himself without a ride. The line of people at the pay phones inside his terminal forced him out into the damp air, where he found refuge in a telephone booth.

He dried his hands on his pants and dialed his parents'

number. Madeline answered and after some soft, comforting words, handed the phone to James.

"Dad, It's John."

"Where the hell are you?"

"My flight was delayed three hours because of the fog and rain. It's a zoo here. I can't get a cab. I need you to pick me up."

There was an ominous silence on the other end of the phone. The only sounds audible were the raindrops pounding the tin roof of the phone booth and a tapping on the glass coming from a man standing outside impatiently, pointing to his watch.

"Dad? Are you there? Hello?"

"Yeah."

"Did you hear what I said? I'm stuck. I need a ride."

"I heard you, Jonathan," he answered indignantly. Then there was an awkward pause. "Are you certain that there are no cabs around? It's really coming down out there. Traffic's gonna be a bear."

"Believe me, if I could take a cab, I would."

The conversation was typical, forced and strained. John was tired of it. He was sorry he had come.

"Well?" he was finally forced to ask. "Can you come and get me or not?" He heard the unmistakable sigh slip through the phone, followed by an obligatory "I'll be there as soon as I can."

John stood restlessly under a cement overhang just outside terminal six. The sound of rainwater rushing out of a busted drainpipe occupied his mind for a moment. But the longer he waited, the more directed his thoughts became. His father. His life with the old man was just a series of moments like this one, a senseless waiting for something that would never come.

He watched curiously through the terminal windows as families reunited and lovers walked out into the cool air, arm in arm, talking about their holiday plans. He turned away and continued to scan the line of cars creeping through the congested pickup areas.

Almost two hours passed. He was back in the same phone booth. "Mom? Where is he? I've been waiting here for two hours."

"I don't know, Johnny," she said to him. "Be patient, sweetheart. He'll be there."

Three and a half hours later, he saw his father's car, sitting off to the side. He ventured out into the deluge. As John approached, he could see, through the wipers' intermittent dance across the misty windshield, his father's hands on either side of an open newspaper. He threw his travel bag on the backseat and slipped in the front next to him.

"Traffic bad?" he asked bitterly.

"No," James answered. "Not especially."

There was an arrested silence. John's eyes focused on the chorus of taillights suspended in the mist. It was always easier, he considered, to talk to him on the telephone rather than face to face. Or not at all. Somehow, it was always easier.

The physical closeness troubled him. It forced him to acknowledge ideas that he'd prefer to ignore. Just looking at him was difficult. Who was this man with the graying temples?

"So, when are you going to stop this foolishness and move back home, John?" James asked, shattering the silence.

"What foolishness?" he questioned angrily. "My life is in California."

"Your family is here, John. This is where you should be, with your brothers. That's the trouble today. Everyone doing his own thing. Then you have to bother with airports and phone calls."

John unfolded his arms and sighed. "Is that what's bothering you?" he asked. "The trip to the airport?"

James shook his head and smiled. "Don't you ever think of anyone but yourself, John?"

He did not respond, as he was too busy choking on the irony of his father's question.

James turned on the radio. The windshield wipers moved rhythmically to the country-and-Western ballads that floated on the air waves. It seemed unusually loud in the car. John was grateful for the distraction. Not another word was exchanged the entire way home.

✳

John finishes his cigarette. He is tired of packing. And these thoughts of his father are distracting. Then there are the letters. He can't stop thinking about them, either. The words in one in particular stand out in his mind: *I save all your letters, Maddie. Tuck them away safely in my pack.*

He goes to his father's footlocker and begins rummaging through the pile of army clothes and assorted mementos. It doesn't take him long to find what he is looking for.

He opens up the green canvas pack. He pulls out a picture of his mom. She is beautiful. And young. In another compartment he finds a plastic Mickey Mouse and blue rosary beads. He shakes his head. It is difficult for him to link these objects to his father.

He unzips the front flap next. There they are: dozens of letters postmarked Roxbury, held together by a dirty shoelace.

Halfway through the pile, he finds an unopened letter. There is no postmark. It is addressed to his mother, and it is from James. He wonders why it was never sent.

He holds it up to the light, trying to catch a glimpse of what's inside. Frustrated and driven by curiosity, he takes a screwdriver and slides the flat head in the fold of the envelope, opening it. It is the most detailed of all the letters.

*

He saw her from an open window on the third floor of an abandoned bank, right in the heart of a German village. She was tiny and not more than six years old. Her platinum hair was pulled back off her face in pigtails, and her eyes, which were either blue or green or perhaps hazel, were big and sad.

James, Leo, and Pearson had just completed setting up an observation post, aware that the Germans were headed their way. Leo went around back to secure the rear entrance. She was in the middle of the littered street below, kneeling over something large and lifeless.

The vision was surreal; he looked, again and again, doubting what he saw. But she was there. A soldier can go days, sometimes weeks, without ever seeing the true casualties of war: streets of ruin, green pastures ripped apart by angry mortars, animals, maimed or killed by indiscriminate gunfire; civilians, particularly children, trapped in a crossfire of inexplicable hatred. It was easy to forget. Easy to believe yourself to be a good soldier, performing a noble service for God and country. If you tried hard enough, you could justify virtually anything you were asked to do. It was part of the code. But when these haunting remnants of life emerged and whispered their demand for recognition, you got rattled and began questioning what it was you were really doing.

"What are the krauts up to now?" Pearson asked, noting James's shaken expression.

"Nothing. I mean, it's not the krauts. There's a little girl down there."

Pearson was not interested. "So what," he said. He continued adjusting the scope on his rifle.

"Well, she can't stay there," James responded. "She's going to get herself killed."

James watched from the window as bricks and cement continued to rain down from the tall buildings outlining the street.

"So what," repeated Pearson. "Not our problem."

"Well, I'm going down there and get her before she gets hit," James insisted. "We can't just leave her there."

Pearson yawned. "Do what you want," he instructed flippantly. "Just don't bring her back here."

Pearson was such a jerk. All he cared about was himself. Like the time they were all assigned to clean a row of houses in a small German town. Pearson went into the first house, followed by James and McNulty. The place was a wreck. There were hunks of wood and splintered glass everywhere. But in the middle of the littered floor stood a beautiful mahogany piano. It was in good shape, with the exception of some bullet holes and a thin layer of dust.

Pearson walked around the house for a couple of minutes, darting perfunctorily from room to room, in an effort to fulfill his obligation. He was finished in less than ten minutes. Having satisfied his responsibility, he returned to the main room moments later and sat down on a wooden crate, placing his fingers on the dusty keys.

"Come on, Pearson," McNulty complained. "Let's get moving."

James leaned his rifle up against the piano and sat down to enjoy the show. Pearson warmed up with some old folk favorites, working the room like some inebriated lounge singer trying to rekindle the lost glory of vaudeville. James leaned his head back and smiled.

"He sure can tickle those ivories," he said, laughing. "Ya know, Twitch, he's really pretty good. But my God, he is just a horse's ass."

After a few more minutes of histrionics, Pearson dove right into the main event. "You know," he boasted, running his fingers up and down the keys, "I'm really a classical pianist," an announcement that elicited a hearty snicker from McNulty, who willingly misunderstood what Pearson said.

"You're a classical *what?*" he laughed.

But Pearson was undaunted. He closed his eyes and let his fingers dance across the keyboard, filling the battered room with the melodic tones of Vivaldi's Summer Concerto.

Halfway through the piece, however, three Germans who had been hiding under the beds on the top floor came racing down the stairs with their guns drawn. Pearson was so wrapped up in his own performance that he never even heard them. James was stunned and could not get to his gun in time. But McNulty was ready. One pass with his machine gun, and he had saved them all from certain slaughter. When it was all over, James threw his arms around McNulty and told him he was his hero.

"Really, McCleary?" he asked boyishly. "I'm your hero? Do you mean it?"

Pearson barely acknowledged him. He just turned around and continued playing.

The memory faded. James bounded down the stairwell. When he arrived, the little girl was perched in the same position. He could see she was crying. He wanted to help but was not sure how. He stood there for several minutes without any acknowledgment from the girl. She was focused on the body that lay at her feet.

"Auf geht's!" he implored her. "Come, little one. Let's go." He touched her shoulder gently, trying to guide her in the direction of safety.

She wanted to stay. She pulled back violently. She looked at him with loathing, her face a book in which multiple chapters of pain and misery could be read. Then she denounced him. "American bums," she said, her tiny voice full of futility and resignation. The words were an earthquake.

"Who is this?" he said, pointing to the body. "Who, who?" he repeated, trying to make her understand. The steady trickle of tears rolling down the little girl's face began to fall faster.

"Meine Großmutter," the little girl said. *"Sie ist tot."*

The dead woman lying before her was her grandmother. She was killed when the company of Americans who were there before them captured the town. His heart sank. This should never happen, he thought to himself.

He turned away and ran into the first floor of the bank. He returned with a tattered curtain he took from a window that had been blown out by artillery fire. He folded the curtain in half. The little girl was still crying, crying tears that were so plentiful they had managed to find their way into his eyes. He placed the worn fabric over the grandmother. He knelt beside her, took her hand and prayed out loud in a sympathetic blending of German and English to the Blessed Mother.

But the war raged on. A mortar shell shattered the solemnity of the moment, leaving James frazzled. His chest grew tight as he looked around for a place to hide her. "What the hell am I supposed to do with a little girl in the middle of a goddamned war?" he wondered out loud.

Up ahead, just a few hundred feet from where he stood, was an old man picking through the scattered debris, placing firewood in a wagon. At first James ignored him, certain that he was hallucinating. How could it be possible? What was this crazy old fool thinking? Shells were falling. The entire town was crumbling. And there he was, placing each scrap of wood he found carefully in his cart. It was bizarre, but he emerged from the dusty shadows at a most opportune time.

James yelled to him, *"Kommen Sie hier! Kommen Sie hier!"*

The man stopped what he was doing. He looked up at James and the frightened little girl, and began walking toward them, unaffected by the exploding shells that were landing all around him. He was calm. His eyes were like two tranquil pools of blue. When he reached James, he placed one hand on his shoulder and held out the other to the little girl. James guided her tiny hand toward the stranger and placed it safely in his wrinkled palm.

"Gehen Sie! Gehen Sie!" he screamed, urging them to leave immediately.

Pearson heard the commotion and came to the window.

"Come on, McCleary," he yelled impatiently. "Leo's back. Let her go for chrissake! We have work to do."

James stood there a moment longer. The little girl turned back a few times, her eyes still burning with enmity.

"Why does she hate me?" he lamented. Then he watched as the joined figures disappeared down the dusty road until the outlines of the two wanderers became faint silhouettes, slipping into the distance. He thought of this, and the little girl's face, as he concluded his letter: *Maddie, how did this kid come to hate me?*

John is spooked. He knows the little girl or knew one just like her anyway. Stephanie Fillmore, his neighbor, five doors down. She was over a lot when they were younger. She was great at checkers. They played all the time. But as time elapsed, she came by less and less.

"I don't think your father likes me very much, Johnny," she told him. "He's always looking at me funny."

At first John said it was nonsense. But after a while, he noticed it too. He stood, arms folded, between his father's chair and the television. "Dad, why do you treat my friends the way you do?"

"What are you talking about, Jonathan?" he answered, craning his neck awkwardly in the direction of the television. It was the bottom of the ninth, the Yankees final at bat.

"You know what I mean," he insisted.

"Jonathan," he said mechanically. "I don't know what you want from me, but I am sure it can wait till later."

"GOD, I HATE YOU! You know that? I really HATE YOU! I hate this house!" he screamed, storming up the stairs to his room, slamming the door behind him. He spent the next fifteen minutes firing anything he could grab against his bedroom walls. Madeline finally came to him.

"Jonathan, knock it off right now, you hear me" she warned him.

"No! I will not! I hate him, Mom. I hate him!"

"What happened now?" she asked.

"He treats me like crap. I'm sick of it! He treats my friends like crap. I don't want to live here!"

"Your friends? What are you talking about, Jonathan?"

His face was red. He struggled to fill his lungs with air. "Stephanie. Does Dad have a problem with Stephanie?" he asked.

"Stephanie Fillmore? Down the street? No, I don't think so. I mean, he's never said anything to me if that's what you mean."

But she knew better. It was something she had noticed too. She recalled walking through the neighborhood one evening after dinner when Stephanie darted out in front of them, chasing a red rubber ball that had kicked off her front stoop and managed to elude her tiny grasp.

"Hello, Mrs. McCleary," the soft voice said.

"Hello to you, Miss Stephanie," Madeline replied, tugging playfully at the child's pigtails.

"Is this Mr. McCleary?"

James could not help but stare as he struggled to qualify the moment that had unexpectedly bridged the gap between present and past.

"Why, yes it is. James, this is Stephanie Fillmore. Our neighbor."

"How do you do, sir," the little girl said, holding out her hand.

James was frozen.

"What are you doing tonight, Stephanie?" Madeline asked, trying to ease the awkwardness.

"My ball," she said pointing to the street. "It rolled into the street," she answered dejectedly. She was biting her lip and looking down at the grass on the edge of the sidewalk that had been torn beneath her restless feet.

"I'm not allowed to go in the street." She paused hopefully. "Can you help me?"

"Sure, honey. Of course we can," Madeline assured her. She nudged James and asked him to retrieve the little girl's ball. He didn't hear a word she said.

"James," Madeline called abruptly. "James," she repeated, shaking his shoulder with her open hand.

He couldn't take his eyes off the child.

"What's the matter with Mr. McCleary?' the little girl asked, alarmed by the vacant stare.

"Nothing's wrong, sweetheart. Nothing at all." Madeline stepped off the curb and extended her own hand into the street, returning the ball to the little girl's eager grasp.

"Here you are, honey. Here's your ball. Now run along. We'll see you again soon."

Madeline was shaken and embarrassed by her husband. "What is going on, James," she asked him. "What is the matter with you?"

He would have liked to have answered her. To tell her about the other little girl he met, and why he found himself chasing and choking on the memory of her tiny, troubled face every time he saw a hopscotch grid or dollhouse. She was a slight thing with blonde hair, just like Stephanie. She was no more than six years old. He would have liked to explain how years later her image still haunted him. Made him shiver. But the words would not come.

He saw her again. She was always there. Never wandered too far. She never left him. The glaring eyes, the twitching mouth. It went right through him. He saw her every time Stephanie was at their house. He saw her after each of his grandchildren was born. She stayed with him on those nights when sleep just would not come. He saw her everywhere he went. Any place where parents or grandparents went to walk with small children, she was there. Looking. At the park, down by the ocean, in shopping malls, and on neighborhood sidewalks, she was there, scowling. She was always there, a restless soul, just like him, sustained forever by the enduring vitality of his memory.

EIGHT

★

When John was eleven years old and began learning about the war in school, the questions came like an assault. He wanted to know things like how his dad managed to sleep outside in the snow. He was curious about things like hand grenades and machine guns. He questioned the reasons for the war and how and why it finally ended. He wanted to know if his dad, the picture of quiet strength, was ever scared.

Then one evening, while James was fixing a leaky faucet in the kitchen and John was doing an assignment for math class, the question James feared most came like a thunderbolt.

"Daddy? Did you ever shoot anyone when you were a soldier?"

James pulled his head out from underneath the sink. He sat up and looked long into his son's brown eyes. He placed his wrench on the floor, wiped his hands on his red flannel shirt, and paused, as if searching for the right answer. "Aren't you doing math homework, Johnny?" he finally said with a weak smile.

"Yeah."

"Well, then stick to math." He picked up the wrench and stuck his head back under the sink.

He did not know what else to do, what else to say. It was the very moment he had played out in his head a thousand times before. He always thought he'd be prepared. Still, the right words, whatever they were, remained elusive.

How do you explain to an eleven-year-old boy that when you are scared and alone, facing the enemy, and looking directly into the eyes of death, you choose to live. How do you let him know that the price you pay for this choice is steep. Extinguishing the light in another man's eyes was the most rudimentary reality of war, yet it remained the worst thing that you could do. No matter how ardently you tried to justify it, to diminish the gravity of what you had done, there was no excusing it. It remained with you forever. So James did what so many other soldiers did when they were asked the same question by one of their children. He lied.

The infantry soldier is an instrument of death. When they were in basic training, Sergeant Billings made sure all of them understood what it meant to be U.S. Infantry: "I don't want any of you cowboys dying nobly for your country," he told them the day they arrived at Fort Custer. "You're no good to us dead. Your job, men, is to make the *other* guy die for *his*."

★

John's question brought James back to that day in Rotgen. On a frigid night in December, he and the entire Ninety-fifth Infantry Division were ordered to protect a company of combat engineers who were removing roadblocks.

James and a squad of twenty men came to the edge of an old vineyard bordered by a stone road lined with brick houses. James and Leo were together as they entered a house adjacent to the vineyard.

They descended a narrow stairwell that lead to the cellar. It smelled like musty wood. The darkness was troubling, but it was not as black as they had expected. There were seven tiny candles on an iron table that illuminated the room, casting peculiar shadows against the wine barrels that lined the gray stone wall.

"Weird," Leo whispered to James.

"Over there," James mouthed to Leo, pointing to the areas between the barrels. They both nodded. They drew their rifles and waited. No one made a sound.

Who had lit the candles? Where was that person now? In an old war manual James read that if a soldier, at any given moment, had to ask himself more than two questions regarding a situation, odds were he needed to begin firing his weapon. He wondered if Leo had read the same manual. He also wondered how much longer he could stand there.

He was preparing to unleash a round of ammo into the dark recesses of the cellar when an elderly man emerged. He was thin and feeble. James laughed, and he and Leo both sighed with relief. The old man seemed to be relieved as well. He smiled and began speaking softly, as if he had been expecting them.

His hands were trembling. His tattered clothing hung on a skeletal frame. He struggled with his English, unable to find the words to make James and Leo understand what he needed. After several unsuccessful attempts to communicate his message, his speech reached fever pitch. He continued to address them in a confused amalgam of German and English.

"What the hell is he saying, McCleary?"

"I don't know! I don't know!"

It wasn't long before he was shouting and pointing to the area between the two largest wine barrels.

"Are there krauts back there, McCleary? Jesus Christ, is that what he's saying?"

"I don't know," James said. "Shit, I don't know! What the hell are we supposed to do?"

"Hey! Hey, goddamn you!" Leo demanded, shaking the elderly German, trying to make him understand their concern.

"What are you saying? What? Who is behind there?"

The German just returned a vacant look.

James had waited long enough. He pushed the man aside and raised his weapon. The old man screamed and an entire family of peasants emerged from the darkness.

The first to come forward was a young boy. He was followed by a dark-haired girl, younger than he, and a woman dressed in a torn shawl who glared at James.

"Peace," Leo said to the woman, placing his hand over his heart. He pointed to James and then back to himself. "We are friends," he continued. "Comrades. Both of us. *Verstehen Sie?*"

Her face had no expression. She asked them if they needed anything. Both James and Leo were cold and tired.

The woman lead them up the cellar stairs. They passed

through a tiny kitchen and up a narrow staircase, eventually settling in a bedroom that faced the road they had just traveled.
The room contained just one bed—a rickety, wood-framed mattress pushed up against a cracked plaster wall. They were happy
to share. They lay down with their weapons and drifted off to
the exchange of whispers coming from the other room.

When they were awakened by the elderly German from the
cellar, James dismissed it as just another dream. Then the yellow light from the old man's lantern found his eyes, and the
sounds of gunfire from just below his window reached his ears.

Both James and Leo peered out at the swarm of Germans
pouring into the vineyard. Some had made it as far as the shed
behind the house, where other members of their squad had settled in. They had already begun shooting at them. Three other
Germans were standing next to a small building directly across
from their window. They were setting up a machine gun. Off in
the distance, they could hear the groan of tank engines. The
Germans were digging in.

"They're taking up positions," Leo screamed. "We have to
move!"

They separated. Leo slipped across to the room next to the
bedroom. James ran back down the staircase into a sitting area
and found a corner from where he could watch the front entrance.

The door was slightly ajar, allowing him to see anyone passing or trying to gain entrance. He was aware that he could be
seen too. The only thing that stood between him and a deadly
date with the enemy was his M-1 and three clips of ammunition.

James sat quietly, thinking about his mother and Madeline
and the candy counter at the Park Theater. He loved John

Wayne movies and Red Hots. He and Madeline always shared a box. They would see how many they could put in their mouths at one time before their eyes began to water. It was only afterward, when a few swallows of soda had squelched the fire on their tongues, that they were able to laugh. But he was a long way from the taste of cinnamon and the Park Theater. The steady flow of German soldiers passing by the door reminded him of that. He had counted eight in all.

It was bizarre. Him sitting there, only a few feet away from the enemy. He was thinking about how he would describe the experience to Madeline. He began formulating the words of a letter in his mind when another German approached the door. He was number nine.

He was a tall, burly man with a full, youthful face. He was dressed in a mountain coat and was carrying a sniper's rifle and a small crate. He stood in the doorway with his back to James. James remained crouched in the corner, begging God to help him. "Our Father, who art in Heaven . . ." he whispered softly, his eyes fixed on the burly German.

He was praying for his life, hoping that God would somehow find it necessary to spare him one more time. Praying that he would live to see another day. He found himself praying for the German too, asking the Heavenly Father to extend a merciful hand and guide him away from the door. "Give us this day, our daily bread . . ."

It was not to be. The German trooper yelled something to one of his comrades and pushed the door open. The destinies of James McCleary and the young German sniper were now linked for eternity.

The German stepped inside and placed the crate on the

floor. He removed his gloves and unfastened the top two buttons of his coat. James's lips continued to form the words of the Our Father as the German reached into his pocket and pulled out a pack of cigarettes. James recognized the box, Lucky Strikes, the same kind Leo smoked.

James continued to watch as the German arched his neck and sighed, releasing three rings of smoke into the frigid air. He was relaxed, happy to be warm and inside, enjoying a smoke. He yawned and stretched his arms. Then he turned to face the room.

He saw James crouching in the far corner. His weapon was pointed directly at him. The German was stunned. He stared at James and James at him. They were both lost in that moment of hesitation when your worst fear takes form in front of you, when time creeps to a virtual halt. It lasts only a few seconds yet feels like an eternity.

The German was the first to move. He reached for his pistol. The sudden movement shattered the stillness. "Amen." James's finger pressed hard against the trigger, and he unleashed a stream of deadly fire, cutting down the young German.

The stunned trooper dropped to his knees. His cigarette fell to the floor as he struggled for one last breath. He clutched his stomach and slumped forward. The echo of the gun's report faded away, and there was silence once more except for the barely audible words of the Lord's Prayer: "As we forgive those who trespass against us . . ."

All around the crumpled body lay the contents of the German's pockets, spilled across the bloody floor: cigarettes, separated from the rest of the pack by the violent intrusion; the remnants of a partially eaten block of chocolate; a brown leather billfold filled with photographs of the dead man's family; six silver coins, the equivalent of two American dollars.

"Thine is the kingdom and the power and the glory, now and forever."

James looked at what he had done. He was sorry. He reached into his shirt, removed his socks and began wiping the perspiration from his forehead. He wanted desperately to explain to the young German why it happened. He wanted to tell him all about Madeline and how they had made plans that just could not be changed. But the big, burly German just lay there, dead.

This horrible reality would touch him again. Outside Rotgen, the first rays of sunlight had just climbed over the clover-laden pastures and wisps of grass. White clouds crawled across a blue sky. All around, the sounds of nature's creatures floated on the morning breeze, carrying with them hope and the promise of a new day. On every flowering knoll and grassy ridge lay the enchantment of a world seemingly untouched.

But the Germans were everywhere, in pillboxes and munition encasements. They buried themselves in the earth, wedded to her in their lust for blood. They waited patiently in camouflaged bunkers and in foxholes, armed with heavy machine guns, mortars, and an unwavering ethic of duty and self-sacrifice, for the slightest sign of the Americans.

It began innocently enough: six of them, crawling up the left flank of a hill single file, their faces inches from the moist earth. They came to rest on their empty bellies just below the crest of the hill. Then the shooting started, coming in from all sides at once.

"We've got to stop," Swinton announced. "Looks as though

they've got a goddamned garrison up there and three friggin' pillboxes."

James, Leo, Pearson, and Erikson all crouched below the bullets whistling over their heads. They were trying to decide what to do before Swinton came up with a plan of his own. McNulty was off by himself, five yards below, cowering behind a ledge.

"Oh shit! Shit! We're gonna die! We are gonna die! Shit. Mother—"

"Shut up, Twitch, damn you!" Pearson yelled back, "or I'll kill you myself."

They all lay there, clutching the ground like orphans seeking refuge in the maternal folds of the earth.

"Erikson," Swinton finally said. "You're best suited for the climb. Crawl up there and get a good look at that bunker. I'll radio the information back to the C.P., and they can start peppering those German bastards with some good old American mortars."

That was all it took. It was Erikson's turn. All it took was a few words from Swinton, and Erikson was going over the top, all by himself.

Erikson looked like a little boy who had just struck out in a Little League game. His eyes were vacant and glassy, and he was uncomfortable knowing the others were all staring at him.

"Erikson," Swinton said, as the frightened soldier prepared to leave. Erikson was nodding, open-mouthed, even though he didn't hear a word Swinton was saying. "Now when you get to the top, see if there's anyone on the left. And if there is, go right. And if there isn't . . ."

★

James thought about the time that Erikson had crept into the barracks and filled Patrick McNulty's boots with a mixture made of shaving cream and red gelatin he had lifted from someone's Care package a half an hour before inspection. While he did this, Michael Thompson, a new recruit, was to keep McNulty occupied outside, in his bare feet, until just minutes before inspection was to begin.

"Now you're sure you got it, Thompson," Erikson asked him. "Do not bring him in until you see the sergeant coming."

"Yeah, Danny," he said. "I got it. No sweat."

Minutes later, Thompson was on.

"Hey, McNulty, check this out," he said, reaching into his pocket and producing three packs of cigarettes. "Are you interested?"

Patrick McNulty's tobacco addiction was no secret in camp. "Am I *interested*?" He laughed. "Are you kidding? Jesus, you really are new. What do you want for 'em, Thompson?"

Thompson looked like he had just stepped out of grade school. The all-American freckle-faced kid from upstate New York. Erikson laughed when he handed him the cigarettes, suggesting that perhaps he'd be more comfortable with a bag of lollipops. He had the kind of face you'd expect to see on a box of cereal or in an ad for soap—wholesome and clean. Still, there he was, a principal player in Erikson's latest scheme.

"Well, McNulty," he replied meditatively, "I really don't know. Let me think about this a minute."

The two men stood outside the barracks, McNulty squirming

to close the deal and Thompson scratching his head, stalling until just the right moment. He waited patiently, feigning interest in the trade as McNulty offered him just about everything under the sun in exchange for the cigarettes. With each attempt he made, Thompson shook his head, until, off in the distance, he saw the faint image of the inspection sergeant inching toward the barracks. He promptly handed the cigarettes to McNulty.

"Tell you what, buddy," Thompson said. "They're yours. Take them."

"Really?" McNulty said. "I can really have 'em? Just like that?"

"Sure, sure. No sweat. Take them. Next time your mom sends cookies, we'll call it square."

McNulty was in heaven. He could taste those Luckies already. But when he saw the sergeant approaching the barracks, he panicked. "Let's get inside," he wailed. Thompson was only too happy to comply.

McNulty passed his palm along his mattress and straightened out a couple of things that Erikson had moved out of place. Then, with little time to spare, he jammed his feet into his boots, causing the slimy mixture to seep in between his toes and out the top and over his laces. They all roared.

"What the hell?" McNulty cried. But there was no time for finger-pointing or retaliation. The sergeant's boot heels were already on the steps of their quarters.

They all stood at attention, Thompson to the right of McNulty and directly across from Erikson. As the sergeant passed down the inspection line, checking everything from shirt collars to weapon hygiene, Thompson's eyes danced recklessly between the mess oozing from McNulty's boots and Erikson's quiet, playful countenance. He was pleased with himself. Just like one of the guys, he thought.

Beads of sweat began to form between the furrows in McNulty's brow, and his lip quivered. It was killing the others as well.

Erikson's plan was almost complete. He observed that Thompson, more than any other, was on the brink of an eruption; he could barely contain himself. It was the kind of thing that Erikson always looked for.

The inspection sergeant continued to move down the center of the two rows of soldiers, settling for the moment in front of Thompson. He sensed his discomfort. "Something wrong, soldier?" he demanded.

"No, sir. Nothing, sir."

Thompson tried to look past the sergeant. But as the young soldier's eyes moved to the area just above the sergeant's shoulder, he caught a glimpse of Daniel Erikson, eyes crossed, nostrils flared, and mouth wide open, revealing two teeth that appeared to be missing, courtesy of a couple of strategically placed globs of shoe polish. Thompson lost it.

"Thompson!" the company sergeant bellowed. "What the hell is so goddamned funny?" The outburst and eventual discovery of McNulty's sloppy boots resulted in a stern admonition and extra duties for both Thompson and McNulty. Erikson walked away unscathed.

★

Daniel Erikson's shoulder was blown apart by shrapnel six minutes after he left the group. It was as if the earth below them had opened up and was beginning to swallow them, one at a time.

They could hear him, lying in a field of clover and weeds, crying: "Mom! Oh God, no! Mom! Those fucking krauts! Ahh! Please God, no!" Daniel Erikson, nineteen-year-old football star from Morrisville, Michigan, was dying. His hopes and dreams were spilling all over the hill. No more jokes. No more games. Just the horrible truth.

"Who's gonna play mama and baby-sit Danny boy, fellas?" Pearson asked.

"Nobody's going anywhere," interrupted Swinton. "The krauts are dug in too well. I will not take the risk. I cannot take that risk. We'll just have to wait."

"Sarge is right," added Twitch, his face a pale, sweaty, contorted mess. "It would be suicide. Yeah. Suicide."

"What do you mean *wait*," questioned James. "Someone's got to go get him. Jesus Christ, Swinton. This isn't some goddamned chapter in a war manual. One of us has got to get him."

"You have nothing to say, McCleary," Swinton commanded.

"It's not right, Pete. I agree with McCleary," Leo said. "One of us has got to get him. You can't let him die like that. Let's put him out of his misery."

Swinton walked away awkwardly like a scolded child, and stood for a moment by himself, away from his men. James could see him on the phone, in all likelihood explaining the situation to someone at the C.P. His inability to step beyond military protocol and lead like a man infuriated James. He waited for him to put down the phone.

"Well, Swinton," James called to him. "What's it gonna be?"

Swinton stomped back to the group, filled with indignation. "Listen McCleary," he shot back violently. "And this goes for all of you. Enough of this righteous bullshit. I am in charge here. And I said nobody's going out there. Getting your ass blown off for Danny doesn't change a goddamned thing. Now fall back and shut your mouths."

"You may be in charge of the group," James fired back. "But James McCleary decides what James McCleary does. You hear him up there? Crying like a baby? Don't be such a fucking robot, Swinton. You sent him up there. Now you either be man enough to assign someone to go get him, or I'm going out myself."

Erikson's moaning and sobbing continued to cascade over the hill. "Oh God!" he screamed. "Help me! Shit! Mommy! Help me!"

It was beginning to unnerve all of them. The others, especially Twitch, just wanted it to end, one way or another. He was chewing his nails and whimpering. James was restless. He had created a divot in the earth where his right boot was twisting restively. Leo was staring at Swinton, hating him for his indecision. His mouth was chalky. He swallowed hard.

"If McCleary goes, Pete," Leo said, "I'm going with him."

"Yeah," Twitch added. "Good idea, Leonardo. Let them go, Pete. I can't listen to it anymore," he said, chewing what was left of his thumbnail. "It's killing me!"

Swinton had heard enough.

"You have nothing to say, Leonardo! Do you hear me? Nothing!" Swinton thundered. "And you go to hell, Twitch, you sniveling sack of shit. This is not about you!"

He paced back and forth, searching for the right thing to say. He could see that James was preparing to challenge him again. "And as far as you're concerned, McCleary, I told you to fall back, goddammit, and I mean it! I will not be held responsible for another death! Do you hear me!"

Swinton had barely finished delivering his edict when James started checking his pack for supplies. Leo was right behind him.

"You *won't* be responsible," he said to Swinton, throwing the pack over his shoulder. "I'm going to make it." He looked at Leo. "We both are. And if we don't and you're still worried about what C.P. will think, just tell him it was all my idea."

"McCleary? McCleary?" he called after him. "McCleary! I'm warning you. You are out of order, soldier. McCleary?"

His words fell hard against James's back. Swinton fired his helmet down and ran his sweaty fingers over the top of his head.

The sky was an azure blue, dotted only by wisps of smoke that hung like icicles from invisible ledges. The sun was bright and frowned on the earth below as angry missiles systematically tore gaping holes in the landscape. The crackle of gunfire and the cacophony of mortars pierced their ears, making it difficult to speak or even think without great effort.

The others watched as James and Leo zigzagged up and across the grassy slope. The Germans were watching too. They showered artillery, spraying the soft earth with streams of fire that rolled across the embankment like an angry wave. The sun, which had slipped momentarily behind a gray cloud of smoke, appeared once more and seemed to settle on their shoulders as they ran, creating the image of tiny angels resting dutifully.

They called back to the others when they reached Erikson, and the group clapped and cheered and roared with laughter. Even Swinton, whose face was still red with anger, was swept away by the moment.

But the victory was bittersweet. The vision of their buddy, a strong, wise-cracking football star reduced to a bloody, whimpering child cut them down worse than the Germans ever could.

James landed in a shallow furrow, half in and half out of a stagnant puddle brown with mud and manure and now blood. The smell settled in his throat. His tongue grew thick against the dry walls of his mouth. He choked on his words.

"Do you hear that hooting and hollering back there, Danny boy?" he finally said, holding back a swell of tears. "That's for you, pal."

"Yeah, big Dan," Leo continued. "It was third and long, big guy. But we made it, just for you."

Danny was shaking his head. "No, no, no," he kept saying. His mouth was dry and his lips were trembling. He called James closer. James could barely hear what he said over the gurgling. "Jimmy," he whispered. "It hurts, Jimmy."

Leo propped up Danny's head with his pack. The two vials of morphine he injected into his thigh were powerful and effective. They wouldn't have to wait long.

"Hey, McCleary," Danny said. "We were always the best at cards. Right, Jimmy?" He was crying, overwhelmed by the finality of what was happening to him. "Pearson says he could take both of us. But you and me, we were always the best."

His eyelids closed, and he swallowed hard. "I was a great quarterback, Jimmy Mac. Did you know that?" He gripped James's hand tighter. His breathing became heavy and erratic. His body heaved and jerked. The gurgling continued.

"Come on, Danny boy," James implored. "Hang in there. You're not done yet. We have things to do. You should see the size of the three roaches Leo and I picked up back there. The big one is yours." Leo grabbed his other hand.

He opened his eyes and tried to smile. "Th-Than-Thanks guys," he said softly, squeezing their hands and arching his back in a desperate attempt to escape the pain. His eyes, clouded by flecks of gray, darted back and forth between the faces of his two friends. He sighed and licked his lips. Then all at once, he was still. James thought of Danny's girl. How she had no idea, and probably wouldn't for several days, that her life had just changed forever. She was probably sitting somewhere, having a soda or knitting a sweater, secure in the fantasy that Danny was well and coming home to her.

Erikson would have liked to have been married. He loved his girl. He wrote to her every day, even when he knew the day's agenda did not include mail pickup. He carried a wallet filled with pictures of the two of them together. They were his most prized possessions, next to his playing cards and lucky marble.

She looked a lot like Madeline. That's what struck James the first time he saw her picture. Her name was Lauren. They were high school sweethearts who met on the very first day of ninth grade in Mr. Vecchio's homeroom class. He sat right behind her. He was always pulling on her long, silky ponytail.

"Do you have a pencil I could borrow," he always asked.

She saw through the ruse but always brought an extra. "Sure, Danny," she always said, smiling after she turned back around.

It was love—innocent, pure, and simple. Fate had brought them together. The burly football star and the ebullient cheerleader. They were the perfect couple.

NINE

★

John's mouth is dry and he is out of cigarettes. He walks downstairs and grabs his coat off the banister. James turns around, startled.

"I'm going to run to the store, Pop, for some cigarettes and a Pepsi. You want anything?"

Behind his glasses, thick and clouded, his eyes glaze and are distant and unresponsive. "No," he replies.

John stands there a moment, awkwardly, before continuing. "Uh, do you think I could borrow your car. It's a little wet outside."

"Keys are in the kitchen drawer," he says.

*

John laughs bitterly as he drives into town. *Can I borrow your car?* he repeats to himself. The words are vaguely familiar to him. He remembers the last time he said them. His father's car is like a time machine: It is exactly the same. Looks the same. Smells the same. Makes the same noise when he stops at an intersection or traffic light, an inimitable squeaking, like sneakers on a gymnasium floor.

He remembers the last time he heard it. It was the night before he left for California. He and his friends were drinking down at Billie's Tavern. Five hours and about fifteen beers later, he walked out into the foggy Rockaway air, got into the car, and was on his way home.

He didn't get very far. He was not more than three blocks from Billie's when he saw two flashing red halos in his rearview mirror.

The police officer brought him home. It was three a.m., but James answered the door after the first knock. They both listened as the officer lectured about the dangers of drinking and driving and about responsibility. James did not say a word. Just glared at John.

After the officer pulled away, James and John were left to face each other. "Well," John began, his breath stale with beer. "Aren't you gonna say something?"

James held his hand out for the keys. John dropped them in his palm. James looked his son up and down: shirt untucked, holes in his jeans, no shoes or socks. "Never again," he muttered. Then he disappeared into the kitchen.

*

John stands on line with a two-liter bottle of soda, a newspaper and a pack of cigarettes. He looks behind the counter. The girl at the register is very pretty. Long blonde hair, soft tan skin and a killer smile. She is young. Probably just out of college. She is friendly too. She smiles at the old man who is in front of him as she checks his order. They chat about the weather and the price of gas. John listens.

When the man opens his wallet, John notices a picture, a family shot with many faces, young and old, all standing around him. They all appear to be happy. He wonders what his story is.

He continues to watch as the old man puts away his change and turns toward the door. John notices the man's jacket—a red Windbreaker with the words *American Legion* written on the back in gold letters—the same one as his dad's.

"Wasn't he cute?" the girl says to him, smiling. "All of those guys are just so adorable."

"Yeah, right," he says, placing his items on the counter.

"Will that be all today, sir?" she asks.

John is still watching the old man. "No," he says decidedly. "I'll take another pack of cigarettes. Please."

He returns home. James hasn't moved. He is still sitting quietly by the window.

"Thought you might want these," John says, dropping a pack of Parliaments on his lap. James taps the tiny box on his palm and removes a cigarette. He clicks his lighter and releases a tiny cloud into the air.

"Make sure you put the keys back in the drawer," he replies.

"Yeah, Pop. Sure." He shakes his head.

He comes out of the kitchen and heads for the stairs. He stops suddenly and walks back to his father. "Oh yeah, I almost forgot," he says, reaching into his pocket. "I found this while I was packing upstairs. Thought you might want to have it."

It is a picture of him and Leo, taken at Fort McCoy. James has not seen it in years. Forgot he even had it. He missed Leo. Thought about him often. Of all the friends he lost, his passing was the hardest.

★

They were tight. After Erikson's death, James was gray, as if all the color had been drained from him. But Leo was right there. He was always right there on so many occasions.

On Leo's nineteenth birthday, he and James requested and received a two-day pass into the town of La Crosse, a hamlet known throughout the barracks for its dance hall and for the droves of horny girls bused in from the neighboring towns. The GI was treated with great affection in La Crosse, particularly by the vivacious young ladies who wanted nothing more than to jitterbug with some of Uncle Sam's finest boys. Leo talked excitedly about what awaited them as they both stuffed their duffle bags.

"There really *is* something about a man in uniform, eh, McCleary," Leo joked as he smoothed his collar in a bathroom mirror. "These two days are gonna be eighteen karat."

James laughed uncomfortably.

"What's the problem, McCleary? Is it your girl?"

"No, no. It's not that. Come on, Leo. I'm fine. Eighteen karat, just like you said."

"Jesus, Jimmy. Loosen up a little," Leo said, reading the true story on James's face. "There's nothing wrong with a little cheek to cheek with a few of Wisconsin's loveliest gals."

The dance hall was bristling with life and the sounds of Glenn Miller, Duke Ellington, and Billie Holiday. Happy feet pounded the laminated dance floor. For two days, James and Leo were swept away, lost in a world colored by music and laughter and the sweet scent of perfumed hair. It was a welcome escape from the cold regimentation of Fort McCoy and Sergeant Billings.

James had a difficult time keeping up with Leo. "Remember what I said, McCleary. Eighteen karat!"

By the end of the first night, James was rubbing his feet and shaking his head as Chris Leonardo "cut a rug" with just about every girl who came his way. Leo was remarkably at ease. He was charming and very smooth. It was like nothing James had ever seen before.

Is this what they teach guys in Evansville? James wondered to himself.

On the second night, James was off to the side again, watching as his friend's assault on the young ladies of La Crosse reached greater proportions. James was smiling in Leo's direction when a beautiful girl with long blonde hair and sparkly green eyes tapped him on the shoulder.

"Is that your friend out there?" she asked softly.

"Yes, yes it is. Why? You want to dance with him too?"

She laughed. "No, but he sure has a lot of energy."

"Yeah. Too much for me. But it's his birthday. I guess he's entitled to blow off a little steam."

"Where are you from, Private . . . uh—"

"McCleary. James McCleary."

"Well, hello Private James McCleary. Nice to meet you. I am Maryanne Sommers."

"I'm from New York, Ms. Sommers. Rockaway Beach actually."

"Are you stationed at McCoy?" she asked.

"Yup."

She moved closer to him and began twirling the ends of her hair.

"I guess you are from around here, Maryanne?" he asked her.

"Sure thing. Live just up the road, about two miles. On that old dairy farm, around the bend."

"That's nice," he said, tracing the curve of her face with desirous eyes.

"How much longer are you gonna be in town, James?" she asked.

"Just tonight. We're due back at the base tomorrow."

"You're going back *tomorrow,* and you're sitting here all by yourself? Why aren't you out there with your friend?"

They both watched as Leo spun around on the dance floor to the sounds of Eddie Safranski, bouncing between two or three different girls.

"Ah, I'm just a little tired. That's all," James said.

They continued to talk. The conversation was light and playful. He was reminded of how much he missed home. And Madeline.

"I'm sure those legs of yours could handle one slow one," she said, grabbing his hand as the fever pitch of the big band artists melted into the soothing tones of a romantic ballad by Sinatra, who was still a young crooner.

Her skin was soft. She smelled like powder, or maybe flowers, and her breath against his neck was warm and sweet.

"Do you have a girl back in New York, James?" she whispered in his ear.

"Yes, yes I do. Her name is Madeline," he said.

"That's a pretty name. I bet you sure do miss her. All this hanging around the barracks with all these fellas. You must get pretty lonely."

He paused a moment, then answered, "I'm doing okay." She buried her face in his shoulder.

When the song was over, Leo was at James's side in an instant. He was eager to meet the beautiful farm girl on his buddy's arm.

"Hey, McCleary. Aren't you gonna introduce me to your friend?"

"Haven't you met enough girls tonight, Leonardo?" he fired back.

"My name's Maryanne," she interrupted, holding out her hand. "It's nice to meet you. But I really have to be going now. It's getting kind of late." She smoothed the bottom of her dress with both hands and turned to James.

"Good night, Private McCleary, and good luck. Take care of yourself." She kissed him softly on the cheek and began to walk away. Then she stopped and turned around. "Oh yeah. If you're ever in La Crosse again, you know where to find me."

Leo's mouth fell open. He was scratching his head. "Jimmy Mac, you dog! Tell me all about it!"

"Are you kidding me, Leonardo. Not a chance. You've had enough excitement for one night."

"Come on, Jimmy. Don't leave me like this! What's the deal?"

James smiled and winked confidently. "It's just like you said, Leo. Eighteen karat!"

✳

It was two years later in Baresna that they found that girl again. Not that girl, but one just like her. James could hardly see her at first. But she was there. The green of her shirt and the melancholy brown in her eyes fought their way through the rubble. She was a young German girl, wounded in the shoulder after an explosion had all but demolished the entire left exterior of her house. He wanted to turn away but could not.

She was a young girl whose eyes whispered softly for an end to her suffering. She looked very familiar, like so many girls he knew back in Rockaway. He was sure he had seen her before. Her name could have been Carolyn or Susan. Or Madeline. He could have been walking with her, hand in hand, over the cobblestone streets of her tiny village. A different time could have placed them side by side under the warm glow of a full moon. But he was an American and she was German, and this world was a world at war. He knew he should leave her, move on to the next house.

They both stood there a moment, looking at the girl, then at each other. They realized it at the same time.

"Are you thinking what I am?" James asked him.

"Yup," Leo said. "It's spooky. She looks just like her."

The resemblance was uncanny. The German girl looked just like Maryanne. James picked up a loose stone and fired it through a window, shattering what was left of the glass. "Goddamn this fucking war!" James yelled. "What the hell are we supposed to do now?" Leo just shook his head.

They sat for a minute. After some water and a few drags on a cigarette, James got up. He grabbed Leo. Together, they began pulling fragments of glass from her face. They poured water from Leo's canteen over her wound. James reached inside his shirt and dressed the area with his socks while Leo began making a bandage from a pale blue tablecloth.

"This is not gonna hold, Jimmy," Leo warned. "It's still coming hard." The wound was deep. She continued to bleed.

"We've got to move her, Leo," James demanded. "She won't make it much longer."

Leo took a quick look outside. "It's long way back to the C.P., Jimmy."

James agreed. There was no time to go back to the command post for a stretcher. She would be gone long before they returned.

So they improvised. They each removed the top of their uniforms and laid them out on the splintered floor, making a kind of bassinette. Cradling the girl, they placed her gently on the makeshift stretcher.

"Do ya think she'll hold, Leo?" James asked, checking their handiwork.

"Well, they're not exactly Boy Scout knots, but we've got a shot."

Leo wiped the girl's blood from the floor and with a stained cloth drew a red cross on both of their packs. "Insurance policy," he whispered to James.

To get there, they'd come across a wide beet field, frosted in ice, and now that field lay between them and the command post. All along the perimeter was the enemy, dug in with rifles poised. Munitions droned off in the distance. James thought about all he had seen. He also thought that just once he'd like to cheat the war the way it had cheated all of them. He prayed that the red crosses would be enough to protect them.

Mortar craters challenged their footing each time they advanced. Every one of their steps had to be taken with great care. But they needed to move quickly. She was dying.

Their legs grew heavy and their arms weary. Their fingers strained. More than once they slipped while struggling to keep the bassinette secure. The thought of losing her now was formidable and equally as troubling as the other thought that hovered over them: Swinton chastising them for helping the enemy.

Then the firing began. Shots came out of the east. *Crack. Crack. Crack.* The Germans had spotted them. James and Leo had come all this way and were less than one hundred yards from their company.

"Can't they see the goddamned crosses!" James screamed. It was not the question he really wanted to ask. He really wanted to know why they were shooting at him. Why, in the name of everything that was fair and logical, was he thousands of miles from home carrying a bloody girl across a godforsaken field of ruin? He really wanted, more than anything else, to understand that.

More shots came from the east. Then from the west. They took cover in a foxhole. The girl was shaking. Her eyes were rolling back into her head.

"We are up the creek, Jimmy," Leo said. "These krauts don't give a shit about this girl."

"Well I do, dammit! We are not staying here."

The girl needed attention. Immediately. They were close

enough to hear the return fire from their company. They could also hear Swinton screaming at them to leave her.

"What now, Jimmy," Leo asked. "What the hell are we supposed to do now?" He wasn't sure, but this was someone's daughter. There were people out there who loved her. There were people who would miss her when she was gone.

James thought about what they were supposed to do. But he followed another voice. They would finish what they had started.

"The captain's gonna snap his cap. Shit, maybe he's right, Jimmy," Leo said, struggling to regain a firm grip on the bassinette. "You know I want to help her too. But what if the captain's right and we get ourselves killed?"

"If the captain's right, Leo," James mused, "then we'll never know the difference."

They continued, dodging the steady stream of gunfire. James could see Swinton and the rest of the company waiting for them. It was the one thing he was focused on when Leo was hit in the thigh by shrapnel from a shell.

Leo crumbled to the earth. James and the girl also fell to the ground. James yelled to Leo, who was holding his leg in disbelief, to stay down. Swinton was yelling too, screaming something about regulations and procedure. And floating gently on the air was the steady whimpering of the girl.

Leo's leg burned. He had never been hit before. James crawled to him. He pulled him over.

"Are you okay, buddy?" he asked.

"Yeah, Jimmy," he said. "Looks like a flesh wound."

James checked his buddy's leg, hoping he was right.

"This is unreal, Leo. What next? Locusts?"

Leonardo forced a smile. "Come on, McCleary," he said. "Wrap me up. This hole's a little cramped for three."

"Okay, Mr. Leonardo," he said, rubbing his hands together. "Let's do this thing." Together, they grabbed the bassinette. Leo staggered to his feet and, with the help of his partner, they carried the girl the rest of the way.

Swinton was the first to receive them. "Goddammit Mc-Cleary! What the hell are you thinking? Do you want to get us all killed? Jesus Christ! Do you know how many goddamned violations you've committed? Do you? What have I told you, all of you, about war. War is protocol. War is precision. War is art. There is no room for any goddamned transgression. McCleary, do you hear me? Are you listening to me, McCleary?"

The girl lived. Leo would be fine. As the medics carried his injured friend off to the dressing station, James smiled because, for a brief moment, he had altered the callousness of combat. But the war raged on. He was still no closer to understanding guys like Swinton and this thing called war. And Captain Peter Swinton and the other artisans of combat were everywhere, just waiting to create their next masterpiece.

James did not have to wait long. His company sustained heavy casualties during house fighting. Thirty-two men in less than two days. Now he and Leo were standing by a railroad bridge, together with these two young boys, replacements, waiting to cross the iron overpass that lay between their current position and their intended destination.

The sky was dark. Behind the structure, a cluster of evergreens, tall and distant, appeared through the rusty slats that crisscrossed all along the upper supports of the bridge. Streaks of smoke melted into the cloud cover, forming a thick, gray ceiling that seemed to insulate the entire area for miles, amplifying the explosions and crossfire.

He hated replacements. They all looked the same. They bounded onto the scene with an unbridled enthusiasm, wearing freshly pressed battle fatigues, shiny boots, and expressions as wholesome as milk and apple pie, all the while quoting Eisenhower or their training officers or even John Wayne. They were young and innocent, ripped prematurely from the vine. They came from intimate neighborhoods all over the United States to training camps and then on to the replacement depots, armed with just enough knowledge to make them a danger to themselves. It was from these "repple depples" that these naive boys came to them; unknown, unknowing, and untrained, thrown unmercifully into the fires of battle.

"Captain, are you sure these guys are ready for this?" James asked Swinton.

Swinton's response was predictable. "They're here, McCleary. In the heart of good old Germany. That means they're ready."

James turned to Leo. "Did you ever meet a bigger asshole, Leonardo?"

They said things and asked questions that only young, unsuspecting replacements would say and ask. All the same things that he had said and asked. Only now he knew better.

They wanted to know where the enemy was and when they were going to see some action.

"Be careful what you wish for," he told them. They never

heard him. They were too eager to prove to the others their worthiness to serve.

That's why he always looked after the new kids. No one else wanted to do it. Swinton was useless, and all of the older guys, even though they knew it was to their benefit to help the replacements, chose to turn the other way. It seemed like every time an entire group was taken out by the Germans, it could be attributed to the carelessness of one of the replacements.

They were nervous and awkward. They bunched up. They talked too much and too loudly. They fired their weapons prematurely. They tried to help, but more often than not, they were a frightening liability.

"When are they gonna stop sending us these fuckin' infants," Carmine Azzaro bawled a few months earlier after one of the new recruits lit up a cigarette during night maneuvers, killing himself and seventeen of the men around him.

"We're going over in two's, gentlemen," Swinton announced. Swinton had been studying the sequence and pattern of the German shelling from his position one hundred yards behind the bridge. The cloudbursts were falling at fourteen-second intervals. Each pair of soldiers, he explained, had exactly fourteen seconds to get across the bridge safely. Timing was critical. There was no margin for error.

McNulty and Pearson made it across safely with no problem. So did Azzaro and Thompson. The next two pairs had similar success. James could tell that as each pair took its turn and crossed over to the other side safely, the anxiety of the replacement pair increased dramatically.

Aware that their time was near, they looked at each other

and back at James, searching desperately for something, anything, to alleviate the overwhelming dread. All he had for them
were words: "Move on sergeant's command," he told them.
"Don't think, fellas. Just run."

But when a soldier was a young soldier and his uniform was
new and he was facing his worst fear for the very first time,
thinking was the only thing he could do. He imagined what his
mom was doing at that very same moment. He remembered the
pattern of the laces on his baseball glove. He wondered why his
legs felt like cement. He saw vividly the white and yellow flowers
that lined the narrow dirt road to his house. He heard so clearly
the sweet, distinct voice of his girl, begging him to come home
safely. He felt her warm lips against his cheek. He considered,
for a moment, what it would feel like to be dead. To fade quietly
into oblivion.

Then the wave of abstraction returned again to more palpa-
ble thoughts, like the taste of his Aunt Lucy's coconut custard
pie or the smell of freshly cut grass on a crisp day in October. It
was all in his head, all at the same time. And then all at once, it
was gone.

"Okay, boys! Move out," Swinton announced.

Now they were racing Death to the other side of an iron railroad bridge. The salt from their tears burned their dirty cheeks.
They prayed to God for fourteen seconds. Just fourteen seconds. Swinton was screaming their names, but their legs were
too heavy to move. They were stuck.

"Delaney, Harper, let's go!" Swinton ordered.

They were panicking. James recognized the look, the glaze
of fear in their eyes. He tried to talk to them over Swinton's

yelling and the cloudbursts, to tell them to wait for the next cy-
cle. He knew they could not make it.

"Stay put, Delaney! Harper! Stay put! Wait there!" James
yelled. He had barely finished screaming when they took off.
They never heard him.

They managed to free themselves, to run. But they were six
seconds too late. They ran anyway, afraid of being left behind,
afraid of being reprimanded, but they were six seconds too late.
When the others, who were watching and counting, reached
the fourteenth second, they were only halfway across the
bridge. That's as far as they got.

James watched it all unfold: the horror, the explosion and
loss of limbs, the cries of pain and desperation, the struggle for
life, and then finally the fading of voices as the bodies tumbled
over the side to the cold metal waiting below. It was the worst
thing he had ever seen.

"McCleary. Leonardo. Let's go! Move your asses!" Swinton
yelled.

They bolted right on time. James ran with his teeth clenched
and his head down, measuring each step and counting each
second. As he passed over the middle of the bridge, he caught a
glimpse through the iron slats of the fallen pair on the tracks
below. He continued to run.

He thought back four days, to the moment the two of them
arrived from the States. Tom Delaney and Chris Harper, from
the same little town in Iowa. They had known each other their
whole lives. They lived just three doors down from each other,
and each boy was engaged to one of the Latzen sisters just
across the road. The parallel direction their lives had taken was

uncanny. They shared everything, from the very beginning, in-cluding aspirations of truly heroic deeds in this great war. They were so young. They were so unprepared. They had only been there four days. Their boots were still shiny.

TEN

★

The winter of 1944/1945 came fast and hard. Most of the 95th Infantry was living in the woods, four men to a tent. James, Leo, Tim Pearson, and Patrick McNulty were thrown together and forced to depend on each other for everything.

Each day, two men from each tent took a turn roaming the snowy woods on maneuvers, looking for German activity, while the other two stayed back and took care of business at the camp. The snow was piled high, and the air was sharp. It was a time all of them preferred to forget.

James wrote to Madeline under a snowy sky in the Ardennes forest. James and his company had been sent there as reinforcements after the massive German breakout that history ultimately recorded as the Battle of the Bulge.

2 December 1944

My dearest Maddie,

It gets more and more difficult to write each time. The conditions aren't the greatest, and nothing much has really been happening. I guess I shouldn't complain, but the monotony is killing me. Even the weather remains the same. It is still snowing, and the drifts are piled high all around us. The sky has been overcast for what seems like weeks, and I just cannot get warm. You can tell a little about how we are living out here by the condition of the envelope. Notice the mud and water stains all over the damn thing. Everything is damp and wet, and it is virtually impossible to keep anything dry. If only the sun would shine for a few days, we would all feel a little better.

It's chow time now. Each day at noon they send us hot soup to keep us warm and to sort of wash down the C rations. It comes in handy. This morning we had flapjacks and prunes and coffee. Last night was steak for supper. We really live out here! (Laugh) The army tries to do as much as it can to keep us healthy although they can't do much about keeping us happy. There is talk of chocolate and cigarettes with the next rations. That should help a little.

Otherwise, things are the same. It's frustrating. And if anything out of the ordinary does happen, as it sometimes does, I can't tell you about it anyway because of the whole censorship thing. All I can tell you sweetheart is how I am doing and that I love you and miss you terribly. I think of you always, especially at night.

I will probably write my mom tomorrow. There's not much for

me to tell her, but I know she wants to hear from me too. Thanks
for your last letter. And the socks! Keep them coming! Until the
next time, I'll close this note with all my love.

Jimmy

While returning back to camp one night from nine straight
hours of field observation, Leo and James, both frozen to the
bone, were looking forward to the warmth and comfort of the
tent.

"Hey, McCleary," Leo said. "Did you get a load of the package that Pearson got the other day? It's hard to believe. I guess
someone *does* love him."

The cardboard parcel arrived on one of the coldest days that
winter, and was filled with goodies from home: salami, pepperoni, chocolate, cake, cookies, cigarettes, and a hollow loaf of Italian bread with a bottle of whiskey safely ensconced in the center.

"I saw it all right," James replied. "But I think that's as close
as any of us are going to get."

Care packages meant everything to them. They were filled
with reminders of the life that was waiting for them just across
the ocean, should they be fortunate enough to be around when
the final shot was fired.

But mail delivery was terrible. Soldiers were disappointed
more often than not. These packages often followed unpredictable, circuitous routes, trailing them from one town to the
next. Many showed up weeks late. Some never reached their intended destinations at all. It was a system so riddled with snafus
that it made the successful delivery of one of the parcels, like
the one Pearson received, all the more miraculous.

James recalled receiving from Madeline a package of cigarettes, hard salami, Hershey Bars, and a plastic bag filled with
seaweed, sand, and a smooth, cream-colored shell. When he
pulled the bag from the box, he was a little confused until he
read the note buried beneath the grains.

Since you can't come to Rockaway Beach,
It will have to come to you.

He stuck his hand in the bag and let the sand fall between his
fingers. Rockaway Beach. He was definitely homesick. Especially when it was cold. Naturally, Rockaway had its fair share of
winter. But at the first sign of spring, the quiet streets and sidewalks awakened from their winter slumber and were transformed instantly into bustling thoroughfares, masses clamoring
for the briny surf. Summer in Rockaway Beach was meant for
swimming, boating, and fishing. It was a time for ice cream, car-
nivals, and long, aimless walks on the boardwalk. It was heaven.
Twelve weeks of sunshine and sand.

Ironically, it was this same sand that he so desperately
wanted to shake off his shoes after Pearl Harbor. He had grown
bored. Unloading crates and stocking shelves at the local A & P
had become tedious. He was only there because his dad had
passed away. Times were tough; the nineteen dollars a week he
brought home to his mother was a godsend.

The A & P was also the place where he met Madeline Brandt,
the prettiest girl he had ever seen. Her face was soft and deli-
cate. Her lips were full and pouty. When she smiled at him the
very first time they saw each other, he fell in love with the dim-

ple on her left cheek, which looked to him to have been placed there ever so carefully by a tiny, celestial hand.

The sands of Rockaway Beach became their playground. The singing gulls were soothing and hypnotic, as was the gentle, salty breath of the foamy surf. It was the perfect place for the young lovers, the place they went most often to run and laugh and dream.

The sand in his hands brought him right back.

"What do you see, Jimmy," she asked, "when you look at the ocean?" She was gazing out at a boat scraping the horizon.

"I see water, Maddie," he teased. "Lots of water."

"Come on, Jimmy," she insisted, amused only for a second. "Tell me what you really see."

"I don't know, Maddie. It's hard to say. He hesitated. "What about you? What do you see out there?"

"That's easy," she replied. "I see endless possibilities. And us. It's all out there. It's simple. Predictable. Like the waves and the tide."

"Yeah," he said sheepishly. "That's exactly what I was going to say."

They both smiled.

He missed her. It was harder than he thought. He was so cavalier when he left. If only she knew the truth.

He remembered telling her he was leaving while they sat on her front porch. "I'm sorry, Maddie," he explained. "You know I love you. Truly. But I don't belong here anymore. Not now anyway."

"You don't have to do this, Jimmy," she pleaded. "No one expects you to."

"I'm not doing it for anybody else, Maddie," he said. "It's me. I need to do it for me."

"I don't understand, Jimmy," she said. "Why now?"

"I'm sorry, Maddie." He wiped a tear from her lashes.

She took a deep breath, trying to gain her composure. "Well, it's probably my fault anyway," she said.

"Your fault?" he questioned. How's that?"

She laughed. "All those John Wayne movies I let you see."

It was a forced laugh. It was a lot to swallow at one time.

"It won't be so bad, Maddie," he told her. "We can write."

"I know, I know, Jimmy," she said. "But it's not the same. What am I going to do without you?"

"Hey, Uncle Sam will probably have me back before you know I'm gone."

She was quiet. "What if you don't come back?" she asked.

"What do you mean not come back," he said. "What kind of talk is that?"

"Come on, Jimmy. I'm not stupid. We have both listened to the reports on the radio."

"I love you, Madeline Brandt," he told her. "I have loved you from the first day I saw you. Remember? I promise. I am coming home to you. And when I do, you will be my wife." They spent the rest of the evening on the porch quietly, wrapped around each other as the crickets serenaded the salty Rockaway air.

James smiled thinking of her, the same smile he wore for days after Madeline's package arrived. That was the power of the package. Madeline always found a way to bridge the miles. Her loving touch was always just a delivery away.

With Pearson it was a different story, and there wasn't much to smile about now. He was heartless. Each time he and Mc-Nulty returned from their tour, he went right to the brown box he tucked away under his cot and began the celebratory routine. Some days it was the salami and crackers. Other times it was a feast: butter cookies, salami on crackers, and a wedge of homemade pound cake. One day, he consumed an entire pepperoni in three bites. He was a selfish slob. No matter what he ate, he never offered them anything, nor did he offer them any whiskey, something he always used to wash down the day's repast. "Warms you right up, fellas," he boasted.

One day, McNulty lifted three cookies from the box. He missed lunch and was worried about passing out. Pearson took one look at him, and the crumbs dancing on his quivering lip, and knew right away.

"Twitch! You sneaky piece of shit!" he screamed. He nearly shot him right on the spot.

"This is ridiculous," James complained.

Finally, after a few especially cold days, James had enough. While Pearson and McNulty were out for the day, and Leo was gathering kindling for the fire they made each night, he stood face to face with the infamous box. It was all there: the cookies, chocolate bars, pepperoni, and salami sticks. There was half a cake left and plenty of crackers too. And of course the Italian bread that harbored Pearson's greatest comfort and James's primary source of anger and frustration.

There was enough liquor for about eight or nine swallows. James picked up the bottle and read the label. He put it back, picked it up, then put it back again.

The temptation proved too much. He took the bottle in his hands and sat down on Pearson's cot with his boots outstretched, mimicking Pearson's histrionics while pouring the whiskey down his throat. It felt so good, warm and invigorating. He planned to take just one or two swallows. But as he lifted the bottle to his lips, the vision of Pearson's gloating face seized his sensibilities, and he proceeded to finish off all but a few drops.

When Leo returned with the wood, he took one look at James's wild expression and the empty bottle, and he knew what had happened.

"McCleary, are you shittin' me? You of all people! What the hell were you thinking?"

"Shut up, Leo," he fired back. "I know. I know. What the hell am I gonna do?"

The two of them stared at each other. Leo smirked. "Did you really drink the whole bottle?" he asked. "Damn, McCleary. You Irish guys really *do* have a problem." He laughed. James picked up an empty metal cup and hurled it at Leo's head.

Leo raised his eyebrows. He opened his canteen, filled the cup and took an old tea bag from his last package and dropped it in. After swirling the water, tea bag, and remnants of the whiskey together, he poured the discolored mixture into Pearson's bottle and placed it back in the loaf of bread.

"Are you kidding me, Leonardo?" James said.

"What choice do you have?" Leo answered. "Well," he continued. "What do you think?"

James sat down on his cot and let his head fall into his open hands.

Pearson and McNulty returned a short time later. James could barely watch as Pearson began his after-hours routine.

"Man, oh man. It was colder today than a witch's tit in a brass brassiere, boys," he announced, removing his jacket and gloves.

He slid the box into sight, sliced a piece of salami, and placed it between two crackers.

"You guys get wood for tonight?"

"Yeah," Leo replied. "I took care of it. We're all set."

"Nice. Hey, McCleary," he continued, the cracker crumbs falling from his mouth as he spoke. "What the hell's wrong with you? Why so quiet?"

"He's fine, Pearson," Leo assured him.

Pearson continued to talk. James was dying. It was only a matter of time.

When Pearson finished gorging himself, he slid the bottle out of the bread and unscrewed the cap. The moment had finally arrived. "Here's to the Third Reich, fellas," he said, lifting the bottle in the air.

Both James and Leo held their breath and shot furtive glances at each other. Pearson brought the bottle to his lips and took a few swallows. He wiped his mouth on his sleeve and slammed the bottle down. James shut his eyes.

"Goddamn!" Pearson exclaimed. "There is nothing in this world like good old American whiskey!"

★

Three days later, they had to abandon the comfort of the tents. They were on the move. The nights in Bastogne were bitterly cold. All James and the others had for comfort was a modest hole in the earth and whatever they could carry from the local farmhouses. On these nights in particular, he thought of things that Sergeant Billings told him. "Make love to Mother Earth" were the words that again resonated most clearly in his ears.

Digging his foxhole was methodical work. After the location

was measured and framed, he placed a satchel charge in the center of the outline in order to blow away the top layers of frozen earth, exposing the loose, removable dirt beneath, which he and Leo excavated with their shovels.

The fruit of their labor was a rectangular hole, five feet deep, two feet wide, and six feet long. These were the dimensions that served them best.

The digging was difficult but kept them warm. Once the hole was finished, the only thing left was to add a few touches of comfort: spare hay or pine needles to cushion the bottom and a log-and-branch roof for protection against tree bursts.

The space was livable but cramped. James always talked of structural improvements: an enclosed latrine or perhaps a sitting area where they could write.

"Yeah," Leo said. "And maybe a front porch and a fireplace too."

He could dream. Writing letters from the field was a problem. It was difficult to find a dry, comfortable place. Still, he managed. The envelopes that traveled the miles were the one constant link between his and Madeline's world. He always sent his love to Rockaway after completing a foxhole.

Once this hole was completed, James and Leo prepared for another night of hardship. As the cold, friendless moon mocked them, they crawled into their hole, wrapped in anything they could find, including rugs and blankets lifted from the farms and tarpaulins stolen from the gunners.

"For the love of God, Leo, are we ever going to be warm again?" James asked.

"Mind over matter, McCleary," he answered, lips trembling. Then he closed his eyes. "Right now, I'm back home, baling hay by the side of my grandfather's barn. It's ninety-five degrees in the shade, and the old man's screaming at me to work a little faster."

James found that Leo's idea worked for a little while. But by one or two in the morning, the biting cold had crept into his bones and no amount of storytelling or fantasizing was going to help. Instead, he found himself thinking of home, clutching phantom images of Madeline and praying for the first light of dawn, trembling in his foxhole like a forlorn kitten.

Morning broke. James's sleepy eyes caught the first rays of sunlight that glistened off the snow-capped mountain peaks in the distance.

"Ah, top of the morning to you, Mr. Leonardo," James said.

"Hope you're not too sore from all that baling you did last night."

"Are you kidding," he answered. "I'm just happy to be awake."

In these early morning hours, most of them stretched and tried to get warm before making preparations for the morning meal. James was different. He sat quietly, removing his boots and the damp pair of socks that had punished him just hours before. He replaced them, in typical fashion, with a second pair he pulled from his right armpit. Then the damp pair assumed the position under his arm. It was a ritual James repeated twice a day.

"First Twitch, now you, McCleary," Leo said to him. "You're nuts, Jimmy Mac. You know that. Really nuts."

James was hungry. He was tired. He had taken his turn with dysentery, but it was the cold that killed him, the merciless cold.

"I can take just about anything this war wants to give me," he always grumbled. "Anything, but these cold, wet feet."

There was still talk of a German offensive. They were all anxious. Their occupation of Bastogne was to be critical to the success of the Allied effort; this particular geographic point, they were told, could be used for a counterattack should the need present itself.

They had traveled for days through the cold air and drifts of snow, their uniforms stuffed with newspaper they hoped would insulate their bodies. They tried everything: layered clothing, blankets, empty oil drums filled with anything that was dry enough to burn.

As those fires burned, rumors spread throughout the lines that German officers had executed American prisoners in one of the other towns. That kindled their hatred.

The Germans were on the move. The Sixth Panzer Division was working its way north while the Fifth stretched its way across the south. They had hit a sector of "green" GIs from the 106th Infantry Division who had just arrived from the States. "Replacements," James said to Leo, shaking his head. They barely had enough time to lace up their boots.

This massive attack by the Germans, a "do-or-die" effort, pushed the inexperienced troops some thirty to forty miles back, creating a bulge in the line for which the bloodiest battle of the campaign would be remembered. Many discussions ensued about General Patton and his military philosophy. They admired George Patton the soldier. But they mocked old "blood-and-guts" Patton, the man.

"Sure," McNulty complained. "His guts. Our blood."

Their work had really only just begun, and the cold was relentless. James and the others continued to trudge up hills and through the snow. Their orders were to make it through the woods to the town of Noville by the following morning.

Pearson and McNulty were the forward observers; James, Leo, and the rest of the group were not far behind.

They had only been walking an hour or so when Pearson and McNulty came racing back toward the rest of the group.

"What the hell is wrong?" James screamed as they came into view.

"Nothing," they responded casually. "Why?"

"What the hell is wrong with you two idiots?" Swinton thundered. "Why are you back here?"

Pearson and McNulty were both laughing.

"Have you two been drinking?" Swinton asked.

"See for yourself, Sarge," Pearson replied, handing him a German canteen filled with schnapps.

"Where the hell did you find this?" Swinton asked.

"Over there, about a mile up behind that patch of trees. Those dead Germans lying in the field had their canteens filled with schnapps!"

"Yeah, McNulty added. "And they certainly are not going to be needing it anymore."

"Christ," James remarked, taking a swig of the potent liquor. "No wonder those krauts were pushing up daisies."

They continued to make their way through the woods without another hint of the Germans. The woods were frightening, especially at night. There were so many places for trouble to hide, they couldn't possibly see them all. The trees were a comfort though; they provided shelter and a place to rest. They stood naked and silent, some misshapen by mortars, like sentinels, watching and waiting. But too many hours in the night forest changed everything.

The moon, as it slipped through the twisted limbs, cast ominous stains across the canvas of snow. Arms. Legs. You just couldn't tell. And on those evenings when the wind was whipping, it took all a soldier had not to shoot at every dancing shadow that caught his eye.

Many nights, when the air was still, they could hear the frozen snow crackle beneath their boots, and wondered if anyone else was listening. They couldn't win. The silence was almost worse than noise. They tried not to think about it. So they passed the time the best way they knew how: ripping on each other.

"Hey, McNulty," Leo said. "I hope you didn't drink right out of that kraut's canteen."

"Why, Leonardo," he answered. "What's the big deal?"

"Did you hear that, McCleary," Leo said. "Twitch doesn't know about kraut canteens."

"What about them, Leonardo," Twitch asked urgently. "What are you guys talking about?"

"Come on, Twitch. Everyone knows what the krauts do," James said, winking at Leo.

McNulty's lip was dancing. "What do you mean?" he demanded. "What do they do?"

"The poison they use," Leo said. "On the canteen rims. Just in case someone tries to use them. But don't worry. It would have to be a large dose to really hurt you."

McNulty ran his hand over his mouth and tongue. James, Pearson, and Azzaro had to turn their heads away.

"Well, how would I know?" McNulty asked. "I mean, if I had gotten any?"

"Usually it takes about twenty-four hours to really kick in," Leo explained. "You know, the effects: stomachache, muscle soreness, that sort of thing. So to be safe, you better watch yourself."

"Jesus Christ," he said to Pearson. "Unbelievable. You had it, too, Pearson. You better watch."

"Oh, right, Twitch," Pearson responded. "Sure thing."

★

Girlfriends. Last names. Shoe sizes. Everything was fair game. James faced a steady barrage of Irish epithets. Pearson took it for his nappy hair. And before he was killed, Neil Hinson was the butt of every joke about rural towns and inbreeding known to man.

Carmine Azzaro was an expert at breaking chops. He was always in the middle of it. But he had a tough time swallowing his own medicine, and it made him a prime target.

Pearson launched the first shot. "Hey Azzaro," he began. "This wind is too much. Can I take cover behind that schnozzola of yours?"

"Eat shit, Pearson, okay? I'm trying to concentrate over here."

"Yeah, Pearson. Leave Carmine alone. He ain't doin nothin' ta you," James said, imitating Azzaro's accent.

They all laughed. McNulty, who was busy testing the joints in his arms and legs, joined the party.

"Come on, Azzaro," he said, leaning back as the moon drew the silhouette of a splintered branch across his face. "No talk of food tonight? Why don't you tell us a little about your mama's beef braciole? Or maybe her chicken cacciatore."

"Listen. I told all of you already. I ain't in no mood. We're supposed to be looking for krauts."

"Yeah, that's right, Leo. Don't mention mommy to little Carmine," Pearson continued. "You know how tightly his manhood is tied to her apron strings."

"What the hell is that supposed to mean, Pearson?"

"Relax, Azzaro," Swinton said. "He's just kidding with you."

"No. That's bullshit. You got something to say to me, Pearson, you big blowhard? Let's hear it."

"All I'm saying, Carmine, is that maybe you and your mom are a little too close. That's all."

"What? What did you say? Is that what you all think? Huh?" They were all biting their lips.

"Ah, fuck yous all," he cried.

*

They reached the town of Noville several hours before daybreak. The group decided to stand one-hour shifts for the remainder of the night.

Everything was pretty quiet. The night slipped away. James, Leo, and McNulty took their turn manning the machine gun at dawn.

"How ya feeling this morning, Twitch?" Leo asked smirking.

"Okay, I guess," he said. "But I'll let you know definitely in four more hours."

The sunrise burned red in a pure, quiet sky. James looked ahead, trying to trace what looked like forest creatures scurrying between bushes. He smiled, until he realized the foolishness of such a thought. It was a platoon of German infantry, advancing in the distance.

James roused the others. Those who were slow to wake were jolted from their foxholes when McNulty opened fire. They sprang to their feet and joined the fray instantly.

The Germans were surprised. They scattered in all directions. Half peeled off to the right. The other half went the other way. McNulty was behind the machine gun, crippled by indecision. The others were shooting from the perimeter of their camp but were relying on McNulty to hold the krauts off with the steady fire from the machine gun.

"Goddamn you, McNulty," Azzaro screamed. "Put some fire on them."

McNulty panicked. The machine gun wouldn't fire. "It's frozen," he cried. "It won't budge."

"What do you mean it's frozen?" James yelled.

"I don't know. I don't know. It won't fire."

"Piss on it, Twitch. Piss on it, goddammit," Azzaro screamed. "I am not going to be taken again."

"What?" McNulty yelled back. His ears were filled with discord.

"Piss on it, damn you. You have to free the mechanism."

McNulty's trembling hands could not negotiate the zipper on his trousers. He fumbled with it until James and Leo took over, showering the .30-caliber weapon from either side. But it was too late. The Germans had them surrounded.

Their faces were red. There must have been fifty krauts in all, each screaming at them to get down on their knees. James and the others dropped their weapons and put their hands behind their heads and their heads between their knees. The snow was cold on their faces. James opened his mouth slightly, and let some of the frozen ground slip past his chalky lips. He could hear them circling, each step announced by the crunching of snow. He could also hear them whispering to each other. His stomach burned. He was thinking of how he was going to stop himself from being sick and praying that whatever was going to happen to them, it would happen fast.

ELEVEN

★

Matt and Paul continue to help John in the attic after work each night. John is grateful for their company; it has not been easy being in the house all these hours, alone with James.

"Johnny, how has Pop been? Any better?" Paul asks one night.

"Uh, I'd say more or less the same," John replies. "Still really sad, distant."

"What about the socks?" Matt asks. "Is he still doing it?"

"Yup," John says. "Every day since I've been here."

Matt just shakes his head. "God, that is weird," he says. "What the hell am I going to do with him after this week?"

The time they spend together invariably leads to jaunts through the more regrettable recollections of life in the house.

"Fighting," Paul blurts out suddenly.

"Huh?" the other two question.

"Fighting—that's what I remember most. There was always so much fighting all the time. About stupid things. 'Watch what you say, Pauly.' 'Don't upset your father, Pauly.' And God forbid you spill something at the table. Jesus Christ! Living in this house was like walking through a friggin minefield."

"Yup, there was certainly plenty of that," Matt agrees.

The two younger McCleary boys continue to exchange horrors from the past. John silently sifts through some old magazines. So often he felt invisible, as if he were part of the furniture in the house. His father looked right through him. His mother made excuses.

Look at me! he screamed in different ways. *Why don't you just look at me?* He often came home with detention slips from school. Mischief in the neighborhood. Run-ins with the police. But in the end, it was all the same. No one was listening.

"Are you kidding me?" he finally says. "The fighting and the nagging was nothing compared to the indifference, the 'Fuck you, Johnny! I don't care' that I always faced."

Matt and Paul look at each other but say nothing.

"You two had a party compared to me," John continues.

"Listen," Matt says. "All things considered, I think we all did okay."

John drops a stack of *Sports Illustrated* into a big green garbage bag. "Are you nuts, Matty? What the hell are you talking about?"

"Come on, John. You're talking about ancient history. That was all a long time ago."

"Really?" he says.

He tells them a story from not too long ago. John was in town with his own family, visiting. It was a lazy, rainy Saturday afternoon. He was sitting on the couch with his son, J.R., in front of the television. The football game he was watching had just ended. He began surfing the channels until he found something to his liking.

The movie channel was running a John Wayne marathon. *The Sands of Iwo Jima* was playing, and he began to talk with his son about the war.

"The big guy there, Sergeant Stryker? He's the good guy. He always wins."

"How come, Daddy?" the child asked.

The sounds of gunfire and soldiers yelling to each other brought James in from the other room. He stood behind them and watched as John continued to extol the merits of John Wayne's character.

"See how strong he is, J.R.?" he boasted. "And brave. Very brave. He's the Duke. A real American hero," he told J.R.

James's face became flushed and contorted. "Why the hell are you letting him watch this crap?" he exploded, glaring at John when he turned around.

"Oh, didn't see you there," he said awkwardly. "You want to sit down and watch with us. You always said I showed no interest in the war. Well, here I am."

James circled the couch and ripped the television plug out of the wall. J.R. was frightened. He was staring at James.

"Why did you do that, Poppy?" he questioned.

"It's okay, J.R.," John said to him. "Go upstairs and see what Grandma is doing."

The little boy left reluctantly. He turned back once to look at James again, then disappeared upstairs.

"Why the hell did you have to do that?" John questioned.

"Grow up, Jonathan, for Christ's sake!" he said. "You think that garbage you're teaching him is war? It's Hollywood, a bunch of political propaganda and nationalist bullshit!"

"Hey, would you keep it down. Jesus, do you want the kids to hear you?"

"Maybe they should," James argued. "Maybe they should know, especially J.R., that what you're telling them is a load of garbage."

"Man, you need to lighten up a little, Pop," he said. "What's the harm? God, it's just a movie. Anyway, I thought you loved John Wayne."

"What's the harm?" James repeated. "What's the harm? The harm, Jonathan, is that people like you watch this crap and then preach it like it's gospel. That's the harm!"

James was pacing the floor in front of the couch.

"What are you getting so worked up about?" John said, getting off the couch to face his father.

"Don't you question me in my house, damn you!" James fired back.

"Oh, that's right. I forgot. This is *your* house. Always was!" John said. His voice was laced with mockery. "God forbid that anyone else express an opinion or get in your way!"

"What? What did you say? I will not stand here, Jonathan, and listen to—"

The screaming had Madeline rushing down the stairs. "What

is going on down here?" she asked. "Stop it! Both of you. Do you hear? I will not have it anymore!"

John walked away. James glared at Madeline. Thoughts of Sully and Erikson and Leo clashed with Hollywood's bastardized version of the war. He picked up the television remote, fired it against the wall, and stormed out the door.

"So what does that all mean, Johnny?" Matt asks. "You had a fight. So what?"

"Amazing," John says, shaking his head in disgust. "You still don't get it, do you?"

★

John has coffee with James the next morning. It has been a long couple of days. His back hurts from the soft mattress he has been sleeping on, and he is tired of the routine and of tiptoeing around his father. He tries to break the monotony.

"Morning, Pop," he says.

James's face is buried in the morning paper.

"Sleep alright last night?" he asks.

"Okay, I guess," James replies.

"Boy, I'll be glad to get back home," he says. "That bed is killing my back."

James does not respond.

"I spoke to J.R. last night," John says. "He called me after you went to bed."

James puts his cup down and looks up from his newspaper, a renewed interest in his eyes. "How is he, John?" he asks.

"Good. He had some news he wanted to share with me," John says. "He's been accepted into the Marines."

"The Marines?" James questions sharply. "What's that all about?"

"It's what he wants to do, Pop. Always has."

James sighs and looks back down at his paper. John puts down his cup on the table a little too hard.

"What's the matter, Pop?" he asks. "Jesus, I thought you'd be proud. He's following—"

"Following who?" James says. "Who asked him to follow anybody? You know what it's like today." He lays the paper out in front of John. "Look at this," he continues. "Another soldier killed. How many kids have we already lost in the Middle East? Horrible. You want me to be happy about this? As bad as it was for me, it is a hundred times worse today."

John gets up and puts his cup in the sink.

"I didn't know we were talking about *you*."

John goes back upstairs. James takes his coffee into the other room and sits in his chair. The news about his grandson has really upset him.

*

"Poppy, do you have any candy?" J.R. asked. He was in town visiting for the summer. They were in the car on their way back from picking up a pizza at Mario's.

"I think that can be arranged easily enough, little guy," James answered, pointing to the glove compartment. "There should be some peppermints in there somewhere."

The two of them continued to talk about school, little league, and the soft chocolate ice cream they would be having after dinner.

"What's this, Poppy?" J.R. asked, searching for a pack of life-savers in the glove compartment. The quest for some pepper-mints had unearthed an envelope with an old photograph of three soldiers peeking out of the top.

"Just an old picture, given to me a very long time ago."

"Is this you, Poppy?" he asked, pointing to one of the three men in the picture.

"No, J.R.," he replied. "That man's name is Tim Pearson. The one on the right is Poppy."

The little boy studied the picture. "Who is the man in the mid-dle, the one with the blue uniform? What is *his* name, Poppy?"

"I don't know," James answered softly. "Why don't you put it away, J.R.?"

J.R. turned his head from the picture to his grandfather and then back again. "You were a GI Joe, Poppy?" he finally asked, his eyes wide with wonder and admiration.

"Yes. Yes I was. But that was a very long time ago."

"Why, Poppy?"

"Why what, J.R.?" he said.

"Why were you a GI Joe, Poppy? How come?"

"It's hard to explain, little fella. But when there's a war, the country needs soldiers to help protect people," he explained. "That's what soldiers do. Understand?"

The child's head was down. "What's war, Poppy?" he asked, continuing to look at the three men in the photograph.

James fiddled with the radio dials. "What did you say, J.R.?"

"I said, 'What is war'? What is it, Poppy?"

"It's a little complicated, buddy. I guess it's sort of like when two countries are mad at each other and the only way they can solve the problem is to fight," he explained. "That's what the soldiers do."

"Oh, like the ones on television," he answered excitedly. "They fight with guns and big tanks and airplanes, right?"

"Well, it's not exactly how it goes," James said. "But, yeah, that's the idea."

"That is so cool," the child said, picking up his head and smiling at his grandfather. "I'm going to be a GI Joe when I grow up. Just like you, Poppy!"

He pulled the car over to the side of the road. He looked at his grandson. The red and white baseball shirt and cap the boy had on was, for a second, replaced by khaki-green battle fatigues and a field helmet. It was a horrible image. It made him shudder.

"No, J.R.," he snapped. "War is bad. Very bad. You will not be a G.I. Joe. Never. You understand? Never say that again."

"But why, Poppy" the boy persisted. You were. And you said that G.I. Joes protect people."

"I know I did," James replied. "I know what I said. But I told you, it's complicated. You would not understand. Maybe when you are older."

"You will tell me about it someday when I'm older, Poppy?" he asked.

James reached for the radio dials again. "Sure, J.R.," he said to him. "Sure. Someday."

★

John has cleared out one half of the attic. There is still a lot of work to be done. He glances at the stack of letters and his father's field pack, resting on the tiny table by the window. He wants to read more, but his attention is diverted by some of the items that remain.

He scans the attic, taking inventory in his mind of all the things he has not seen for years. He is looking at the oak crib that has been in his family for generations. It is the only real McCleary heirloom.

When J.R. was born, James and Madeline made the trip out to California to celebrate the birth of their first grandchild. Although James had refused for years to travel to California, the appeal of his grandson was too much to resist.

John was standing next to his father, looking through the nursery window in awe at the tiny life that his wife had just brought into the world. He was not sure what to feel.

He was thinking that this could be the opportunity he had waited for his whole life. Something. Anything. How could it fail? How could this man, now a grandfather for the very first time, gaze out at all those tiny, angelic faces adrift in a veritable sea of pink and blue and not feel the need to talk about sons and fathers? And regrets and apologies? Even James McCleary, the last bastion of stoicism, was no match for such an emotional tidal wave. It seemed as though it might all work out okay, but he was not sure if he had the energy, or desire, to try.

"Congratulations, *Dad*," James said, placing his palm on his son's shoulder.

John smiled, all the while watching the rhythmic rising and falling of the powder-blue blanket covering his newborn baby boy.

"Lots of babies in there," James continued. "Stork must have been working overtime last night! Amazing. Really. Which one is ours, Johnny?"

"First row on the left, second one in," he answered. "Right next to the Mendelson girl."

"Ah, he's beautiful, Johnny. Just beautiful." He paused to take another look. "Tell me. I'm dying over here. What's his name?" James asked.

"John. His name is John Robert McCleary, Jr. We're going to call him J.R."

"Really? That's great!"

James was unusually expressive. "You know, Johnny, your mother and I were talking on the way over here. We would like you to have the crib, you know, Grandma's crib, the one up in the attic?"

"What do you mean, Dad?" he answered uncomfortably.

"For the baby. A baby needs to have a crib, right?"

There was an awkward silence.

"Yeah, Dad. I guess so. But Michele and I already bought one," John explained.

"What?"

"We already bought a crib," he repeated. "Weeks ago."

James turned away. His eyes were fixed on his grandson. An uncomfortable silence followed.

"Hey, I appreciate that, Dad," John said. "Really. But I don't need it. If it's all the same, I think I'll pass."

"Okay, Johnny. Fine. That's just fine. I don't give a good god-damn what you do. It doesn't matter to me. I just thought that maybe it would mean something to you. That's all."

"What means something to me, is that you are actually here," John tried to explain.

James turned and walked away from the window.

"Did you hear what I said, Pop?" he asked. "Pop?"

★

Baseball cards. Old suits. Dusty record albums and athletic trophies. It is all there in front of him, most of it divided neatly into cardboard boxes. His life. Each object in the attic tells its own story.

There is good and bad, success and disappointment, joy and resentment. So many of the painful chapters are tied up with his father's absence: father-and-son day at the elementary school, when he failed algebra and had to attend summer school, when Stephanie Fillmore chose to go to the prom with Anthony Marro instead of him, the time he came home drunk, begging for acknowledgment, only to have the man he needed turn his back on him.

He reaches into the pile. He has not seen his baseball glove in many years. He pulls it from one of the boxes marked "Johnny." It is flat and shapeless. He puts it on his hand, spits in it, and pounds his fist into the pocket. It is much too small. The leather is faded and dry. He can barely make out the word *Spalding* on the back and the initials *J.M.* scribbled across the heel in red Magic Marker. But the picture is vivid and the voices are strong and clear.

He was eight years old. It was a cool evening in August. The sun had just dipped below the trees out in center field at Fireman's Field, and nightfall was not far off. There was a murmur of excitement coming from the stands behind the Rockaway dugout. "Come on guys," the coach screamed. "Just one more out!"

It was the final game of the Little League World Series. The score was 9–8. The team from Roxbury had the bases loaded, and there was an 0–2 count on the batter.

The pitcher delivered the ball. As it left his hand, everyone seated behind the backstop could see that it was destined for the catcher's glove; a fastball that would split the plate right down the middle and bring the championship home to Rockaway.

John was standing in right field, hands on his knees, dreaming of darting across the field once the third out was recorded and joining the jubilant pile-on at the pitcher's mound. He could hear the laughter and the raucous cheering: "We are number one! We are number one!" His smile could be seen from anywhere in the park.

But the image was fleeting. The unmistakable "ding" that is made when a baseball is struck by a metal bat jolted him from the daydream.

It was a high, looping fly ball curving toward the right-field line. John did not see it. He looked up into the evening sky. The pounding of his heart had climbed and settled in his throat as the image of nine delirious eight-year-olds was replaced by a picture of long faces and tear-stained cheeks. It was a desperation he had never felt before.

His thoughts turned instantly to his parents and brothers, friends and neighbors. They were all seated in the stands watching.

"I have to catch this ball," he whispered to himself.

All was not lost. The ball emerged miraculously from behind a thin line of clouds that appeared to be sitting just above the bleachers. There was still enough time.

John raced toward the spot where it was likely to land. He

could feel his cleats tearing up the soft outfield grass. His glove was extended as far as it could reach. "I'm gonna get there," he whispered again. "I'm gonna get there."

He was running full tilt. His hat was lying in the grass somewhere behind him, and his thoughts had returned to the picture of victory and glory.

The ball began its descent. The red laces were spinning right above him. He opened his glove and the ball plunked down right in the center of the yawning pocket. He had made it! It felt so good.

But before he could squeeze his glove shut, the ball slipped out and rolled helplessly into a patch of clover several feet beyond the foul line. There was a collective groan. Then, shortly afterward, painful condemnation.

"Oh, how could you, McCleary! It was right in your glove. How could you miss it? You cost us the game."

"What are you crying for?" his father asked him on the way home.

"We lost the game," he responded indignantly. "Weren't you watching? We lost. And it's all my fault."

"I still don't understand why you're crying," James said.

"Because we lost! It was the most important game of the year. I should have caught the ball. I blew it!" He was sobbing. Tears were streaming down his cheeks.

"It's just a game, Johnny," James said. "It doesn't matter."

"Yeah," he screamed back. "It matters to me!"

His father continued to drive the car, looking ahead at an elderly man standing on the sidewalk screaming at a storekeeper to open the doors for him even though it was ten minutes past closing.

"Stop being a baby, Jonathan," he said, turning to face his son. "There are worse things in life than losing a baseball game. Save your tears for those."

John is looking at the glove through teary eyes. He pounds the pocket with his fist. Then he takes it off his hand. He looks at it once more, shakes his head and tosses it back into the box.

Just to the left of the box marked "Johnny" is another with the words *Christmas Decorations* scrawled across the top flap. It is filled with tinsel, decorative bulbs, handmade ornaments, an assortment of Santa Claus figurines, and, of course, plenty of lights, Christmas lights. What a fiasco, John thought. Every year, right after Thanksgiving, the tension in the house would build, boil, and bubble like magma right before a volcanic eruption. The expectation of decorating for the season trailed James for the entire month.

Madeline loved to decorate for the holidays. James saw it as a bother, an unfortunate glitch in the comfort of his day-to-day routine. She took care of the inside all by herself. Out of necessity, she had developed a routine of her own.

A Christmas record, for starters, usually something from Bing Crosby or Perry Como, just to set the mood. Then came the Christmas cookies in the oven and fresh logs for the fire. After exchanging a jingle bells apron for her favorite snowflake sweater, she would begin her holiday assault on the house, stringing a garland in each doorway and placing crocheted snowmen and pinecone reindeer on every shelf and tabletop.

When the interior had been transformed to her liking, she turned her attention to the outside.

"James, I'd like the lights put up on the house," she'd ask. He would huff and puff and offer some resistance, citing other jobs he had to do that could not wait. She would follow him around, unwilling to accept his indifference. Ultimately, her persistence won out, and he would climb the stairs to the attic, grumbling about commercialism and electric bills, until returning with the box in his hands.

It was John's job to help, one of the many "perks" associated with being the oldest. The smell of cardboard and the sight of those lights rekindle the glory. "Hold the damn ladder still, Johnny, for Christ's sake. What are you trying to do, kill me?"

God, how his father hated Christmas. Probably more than anyone he knew. That's why one of his letters to Madeline is so puzzling.

24 Dec. 1944

Dear Maddie

I just finished building my home so I have a chance to write. It just started to snow again, just a light fall. Leo and I are sharing a 4 X 6 well, covered over with logs and lined at the bottom with hay. It is cramped. We have not had hot water since we left the last town, where the people were so good to us. As a result, we have also not had a razor to our faces in quite some time.

The area is covered with snow, and the sky is overcast. It gets damp and cold, especially my feet, when we aren't working. But that can't be helped. I tell you Maddie, if only it weren't Christmas, I would feel much better. You know how much I enjoy all the festivities. What I wouldn't give to be sitting with you by your tree, sipping warm cider and stringing popcorn. A little Christmas music wouldn't hurt either! It is lousy. Next year, I promise, we will celebrate this wonderful day the way it should be.

We ran into some Germans today. Let's just say it was not

what I expected. And not something that should happen on this
sacred day. It's been a long day. I am tired. Merry Christmas, my
darling. I mailed your present. I hope you like it. I am wearing
yours, right now, on my feet. Thank you.

All my love to you. Give my love to your folks as well.

Jimmy

John wrestles with the incongruity of the letter. James Mc-
Cleary, enjoying holiday festivities, drinking warm cider, and
stringing popcorn? How could it be? The man who made Ebe-
neezer Scrooge look like Burl Ives, a lover of Christmas? It
didn't make any sense. Of course, the letter was incomplete.
That Christmas Eve, James McCleary did not tell Madeline the
whole story about those Germans.

The snow in the field had turned to ice. It crunched beneath
their boots, this under a cold, pale blue sky and under a sun
that slanted through the black branches of the trees lining the
field. The glare rising from the snowy blanket hurt their eyes
and seemed to linger in the thick, frigid air, giving the whole
scene a mystical quality.

In the middle of the field a Tiger tank smoldered, black,
busted, and silent. It sat like a wounded animal, waiting to die.
Its punctured engine hissed at them, the only sound audible
through the frosty air.

"McCleary, you and Leonardo take five guys and head out
into the field and check out the tank those mortars just dis-
abled," Swinton ordered.

They approached cautiously, uncertain as to the whereabouts of the German crew.

"Some Christmas, eh McCleary?" Leo remarked. "You don't

suppose that kraut tank has any eggnog now, do you?"

Their feet were heavy as they walked through the frozen field, spooked by the calm before them. Most of them were feeling bad about being away for the holidays. All they wanted to do was go back to camp and drink themselves stupid, to forget for a little while.

About halfway between their post and the German tank, a metallic groan pierced the stillness of the afternoon, and the turret swung open. Each of them drew his gun and, with their breath visible before them, prepared to fire. They stood still, focused on the hole that sat atop the tank. The only sounds they could hear were the hissing and the plaintive cry of a bird up above. Then they heard the sound of laughter, their own, as they saw, rising out of the turret and waving in the Christmas breeze, a white flag fashioned from a piece of tattered cloth.

They advanced now with lighter steps. *Crunch. Crunch. Crunch.*

"Man, oh man," Leonardo uttered. "That is one sweet sight. Thank you, Santy Claus."

James instructed the others to follow his lead. They snaked their way through the thickets and toward the Germans. The talk returned to more pleasant matters. "So, when we get back to camp, Pearson," Leo said, "we'll meet at your foxhole. I'll bring my bottle, and we'll mix it with yours. And with any luck, the krauts might have a little present for us as well."

"Cut the shit, you two," James warned. "We need to let them know we're here."

They were just about to call out to the German crew when the tube on the tank began to rotate toward them and then fired, tearing large holes in the soft earth and scattering the entire squad.

"Put some fire on that goddamned thing!" James yelled to the others.

Once they responded, peppering the tank with everything they had, the tank fell silent again. Then the entire German crew came pouring out of the escape hatch, hollering "comrade!" "*frieden erklaren!*" and "*froehliche Weinachten!*" They held their hands high over their heads. They were crying. One of the men had vomited all over the front of his uniform.

James continued to scream, "Put some fire on them!"

Leo and the others pulled back.

"Jesus Christ," Pearson said. "Did they just wish us a Merry Christmas?"

They all laughed, but James pushed past and began firing at the line of helpless soldiers, cutting them down. They flopped over like rag dolls. Leonardo called to him, but he was somewhere else. Never blinked his eyes. It lasted just two minutes. Then the results of the fit lay all around them: a six-man German tank crew all dead.

They were all speechless. They hung their heads.

"McCleary," Leo finally whispered. "Hey man, are you okay?"

James looked down at his right pant leg. It was soaked with urine. "Yeah, Leo. Yeah. Sure. I'm okay."

A frigid wind whipped across their faces. They turned and headed back for camp. It was Christmas Eve. And there was supposed to be a celebration at Pearson's place.

TWELVE

⭐

I hope none of that crap in those garbage bags is mine," Matthew warns playfully as he catches his brother on one of his trips from the attic to the curb.

"Relax," John replies. "I haven't even seen anything that belongs to you."

"Where is he?" Matt asks, jingling his car keys nervously.

"Out in back, on the porch. How's everything going over at your place?" John asks. "Will you be ready for him on Friday?"

"Should be," Matt says. "Just have a few odds and ends to pull together."

The two of them walk toward the house together, marveling at the junk they have amassed over time.

"Come across anything worth saving?" Matt says.

"What do you mean, Matt?" he answers curtly.

"Things. You know, baseball bats, old report cards, year-books. That sort of thing."

"I don't know," he answers. "I found some good stuff, I guess. Mostly junk though."

He considers telling him about the letters. Maybe Matt would like to see them. But he decides not to. He is not sure why.

There is one in particular that bothers him. Actually, it isn't a letter; it's a postcard he found mixed in with the pile. It seems to have been misplaced. The writing is a lot smaller and difficult to read. There is no date. He realizes only afterward that it is from a German prison camp.

The card is small, there is not much written on it. John reads it over several times, searching for something he may have missed.

Dear Maddie,

Was captured by the Germans. I am being held in a small room. It is dark and the walls are close, but I am okay for now. I do not know what to expect. No matter what happens, I love you. Tell my mom not to worry and that I love her too. I don't think I'll be allowed to write again.

Jimmy

★

Most of them had never seen the enemy up close. They had only heard the stories. As the German officers approached, they did not appear to be ogres. They seemed unusually calm and human, much like the young German he and Pearson had captured back in Paderborn. Cigarettes dangled carelessly from their lips. They were laughing. It made him wonder. There were about five or six of them, all there, in the icy field where the distant cry of birds seemed to acknowledge the Americans' misfortune. They strutted back and forth, continuing to smile, their steel-blue uniforms stark against the backdrop of white. One in particular had that look of a bastard: that frosted Germanic silver hair—premature, it looked like, since he couldn't have been more than forty. He had an iron jaw and piercing eyes that matched the color of his jacket. He passed in front of them several times with a pensive look, as if he were preparing something in his head. Then he stopped and began berating the entire group, one soldier at a time. He sneered at them. Spit on them.

"Amis shit," he announced, pulling a pistol from his holster. "German SS God's soldiers." Then he began shooting every other American in the line, stopping when he got to James. Dominic Scotto. John Kinsley. Robert Geraghty, Jr.—all dead. Now he fixed his eyes on James.

He was big and mean. He stood in front of James, speaking to him in short, abrupt phrases. Each word brought foul breath, the breath of a smoker on half rations. It was the last thing James remembered before the German's revolver whipped him on the left side of his head.

Hours later, he found himself in a small cell. He was officially a prisoner of war. Do not show your weakness, Jimmy, he told himself. Don't ever show your weakness.

He knew neither the time nor the date, but it was January 17, 1945, eight a.m., when heavy footsteps in the hall preceded the appearance of a heavy-set, elderly SS guard in his doorway. The man had chubby red cheeks, and spectacles dangling off the end of his nose. He looked like a plump schoolteacher crammed into a snazzy uniform. He seemed a bit unsure of himself as he presented himself to James. Even his orders came out a little hesitant.

"Come with me, please," he said in near perfect English.

He led James down a narrow corridor and into a much larger room. There were paintings on the walls, and Nazi insignias emblazoned on flags that hung from polished brass rods.

The same officer from earlier—the one who had executed his friends—waited for him there and told him to sit down. "We are stronger than Americans," he told him. "Better suited for war." He boasted that he could hold his breath under water for five minutes at a time. He rolled up his sleeve and flexed his tattooed bicep, bragging about being able to lift three times his own body weight. He spoke of German technology and ingenuity. Then the questions came.

"Where is staging area, Ami?" he demanded.

"James McCleary," he replied. "Corporal, 44-006-019."

The officer cocked his head and smirked. "Ami, tell me where the staging area is," he repeated.

"James McCleary, Corporal, 44-006-019."

"Listen to me, Ami," the German continued, burying his massive forefinger in the center of James's chest. "One last time. Tell me where the staging area is."

"Geneva convention," James replied. "James McCleary, Corporal, 44-006-019."

The big German smiled. "Geneva Convention" he repeated, mocking James. "Ami is a boy." He laughed out loud.

The officer turned his back to James. He walked with deliberation to the opposite side of the room, then turned again to face his prisoner. He pulled a map from his breast pocket and placed it down in front of James. His face softened.

"Which town, Ami?" he persisted. "We know of plan to attack. We know all about the major offensive. Your comrades have already told us the when and the where, but I think it would be appropriate if you told too." He smiled and placed his hand gently on James's shoulder. He offered him a piece of candy. "So tell us," he said. "Show us now. Point to staging area."

James shook his head no.

Minutes passed. Then, back in his cell, days passed. He felt himself weakening. But it wasn't the interrogation or the tight, oppressive surroundings that threatened to undermine his resolve. It wasn't the slices of sawdust bread laced with grease drippings. What knocked him back and nearly destroyed him was the penny postcard given to him by the German officer.

All of the prisoners received one. A simple, white card, three inches wide and five inches long, on which they were instructed to place their most intimate thoughts. It was to be their only correspondence home. A space no bigger than the palm of a human hand. Unreal.

For James McCleary, a boy who had spent the majority of his young life playing in the surf of Rockaway Beach and shooting foul shots in the high school gymnasium, five inches of cardboard was an assault. He wrote with great difficulty. The smell of the interrogation room made him nauseous. The officer had left the candy and some cigarettes on the table where James sat. James wondered if he'd be back.

After a time by himself, James was placed back with the others. He was happy to see friendly faces. Together, they struggled. They were tired. They were hungry and thirsty. They had been stripped of their uniforms, their hope, and their dignity. They had lost all contact with the world outside.

The days were endless. To pass the time, they exchanged funny stories, some of which had never been told before. Patrick McNulty told about the time that he mistook Neil Hinson's foxhole for the latrine and shit on his head.

"Boy, was he mad at me. Made me trade foxholes with him right there in the middle of the night. Also cost me three packs of cigarettes. All in all, I have to say, I think it was worth it."

"You are an asshole, Twitch," Azzaro said. "You know that?"

"Hey, easy, Carmine," James said. "He's just trying to pass the time."

"Well, what kind of fucking story is that?" he continued. 'Shit in a foxhole. That's what we're sitting in right now. I don't want to hear that!"

"Well, let's hear what *you* got, dago," Pearson remarked. "Make us all feel better, Azzaro."

Carmine Azzaro loved to talk about his girl, Maryanne Lupoli. The way he talked, you would think she was some pinup girl, every GI's fantasy. Strange though. None of them had seen a picture yet.

"So," Azzaro began, "Maryanne's in the basement of the bakeshop. Every night, an hour before closing, old man Alonso sent her down there to prepare the bread trays for baking the next day. You know, clean 'em, stack 'em up."

"Come on, Azzaro," James complained. "Not another food story."

"Yeah, Azzaro," McNulty said. "This is definitely not the time."

"Would you let me talk here, goddammit," Azzaro complained. "Jesus, you guys are unbelievable." He uncrossed his legs and locked his hands behind his head. Then he smiled. He explained how before he went to work at the butcher shop, he stopped in to see her. She always managed to slip him a fresh roll, éclair, or muffin. Azzaro licked his lips as he described the melted butter and fresh cream filling.

The others groaned.

"All right, all right," he said. He continued his story.

That morning, Maryanne handed him a hot roll with a note stuffed inside: *Meet me by the cellar door at six,* it said, with a little heart next to the six. Turned out that old man Alonso was knocking off early that day.

In their damp drafty room, they were all listening to Azzaro detail every minute leading up to the incident. It was insufferably dark; the only two windows in the tiny cell had been painted black. They sat on the cold, concrete floor—James, Pearson, Azzaro, McNulty, Leonardo—all huddled together. It was the only way they could keep from freezing. But after a few hours on that floor, their backs ached, and their legs began to numb. It was hard not to be able to stretch out. Even harder not knowing exactly where they were and what was going to happen next. But listening to Azzaro weave his tale was a nice diversion.

"So, long story short, we're lying on the table," he said, "doing our thing, when her leg swings off to the side and knocks an entire stack of metal bread trays onto the concrete floor. Man, you should have heard the noise. You would have thought the whole place was crumbling. The two of us couldn't stop laughing."

The entire group was smiling, even Pearson. Azzaro paused

for a moment to catch his breath. Then he explained how down the stairs, unexpected, came old man Alonso, who had come back to the shop to get something he had left behind. He took one look at Azzaro, pants around his ankles, and picked up the nearest thing he could find—a shovel—and chased him right out of the store.

They laughed uncontrollably at the image of Azzaro, with his pants around his ankles, being chased out of a basement by a man with a shovel. James had tears in his eyes, and McNulty was doubled over.

"Good one, Azzaro," Pearson said. "The thought of you running with that little sausage of yours swinging in the breeze is absolutely hilarious."

It was good to laugh. It took their minds off the horrors that awaited them.

"Hey, McCleary. Why don't you tell your transport story?" Leo said. "I don't think everyone here knows it."

"Aw, I don't know, Leo," he said. "Azzaro's a tough act to follow."

"Yeah, Leonardo. How's he gonna beat what we've heard so far?" McNulty questioned.

"Are you kidding me?" Leo continued. "It's a great story."

James got up and crossed the small concrete slab to the other side of the cell. He stood at one of the windows, trying to chip some paint off the glass. He was desperate for some natural light, a glimpse at the world they had not seen in days.

The air was cold and close. It also had begun to smell, a musty odor, like stagnant puddles on a dirty street. He really did not want to listen to any more stories and certainly did not want to tell any. He felt like curling up next to the large, wooden crate that sat below the other window. Maybe some sleep would help. But the others would not be denied.

When James was at Fort Custer in Louisana, before he got to McCoy, the company commander called him into his tent. He showed him a map and told him that as part of his training, he had to pick up a load, bring it to another camp and then return safely.

"What am I going to pick up?" James asked him. The commander told him that he would find out when he got there.

James drove to the warehouse and backed up the truck to the loading platform. He told the guy standing there that he was from truck company 3805 and that he was picking up a load. He found out that this "load" he was to transport consisted of several crates of dynamite. James was not pleased.

"I don't want any dynamite," he said. "No way!"

The man told him that there was nothing to worry about, that it wasn't dangerous. After warming his hands over a fire in a fifty-gallon drum, the nut took a stick of dynamite from an open case on the loading platform and broke it in half. Threw it down. Jumped on it. Threw it against the wall. Nothing happened. Then he took the two halves of the stick, and the crazy son of a bitch threw them into the drum. Aside from a flash of fire, still nothing.

"Jesus Christ, Leonardo," Azzaro whined. "This is the story you wanted us to hear?"

"Relax, Azzaro," Leo said. "He's getting to the good part."

James explained that after they were done loading up, the man started to place these banners with big red letters on each side of the truck. DYNAMITE. On the front of the truck. DYNA-

MITE. On the back of the truck. DYNAMITE. Then he put about ten red flags on the truck as well.

James was curious. "Excuse me," he said. "If it's not dangerous, and I have nothing to worry about, why all the banners and flags?"

"Don't sweat it, soldier," he assured James. "It's just procedure. The law around here. You can't haul explosives without them." It seemed logical enough.

When he finished with the banners and flags, James was pretty satisfied. He had just one question. "Well," he asked. "How *do* these things explode?"

"You have to use detonators," the man explained. "You take five sticks and tie them together. Put a detonator in each stick and run a wire to a generator a safe distance away and then push the plunger. *Bam!* It's that simple."

James hopped up in the truck. He was all set to pull out. But the man stopped him. Tossed James a heavy burlap sack, loaded mostly, it seemed, with padding.

"What's in here?" James asked.

"The detonators," came the answer.

"Are *these* dangerous?" James asked him.

"No," he told him. Then he smiled a little and said, "Well, they're not dangerous, unless you drop them."

James placed them gently on the seat next to him, holding them down each time he hit a bump or made a sharp turn. He was driving along for about an hour, holding the detonators, when all of a sudden he saw this hayseed standing on the side of the road—straw hat, overalls, the whole bit—with his thumb out. James couldn't believe it. All these goddamned dynamite signs and red flags, he thought to himself, and this guy wanted to ride with *him?* He stopped the truck.

"Where you headed, friend?" he asked him.

"About ten miles up the road," the hitchhiker replied. James asked him if he was sure he wanted to ride with him. The stranger smiled and jumped in.

As soon as he got comfortable, James handed him the box of detonators. Told him to hold it on his lap. "Don't shake it," he said. "It's very valuable."

Azzaro held back a smile, determined not to give Leo and James the satisfaction.

They were driving along, and James was feeling much better, a lot safer. The stranger started spilling his guts to James about his lousy childhood and how he never learned to read and write, and about his girl in Chatanooga. Blah, blah, blah. It all started to make sense. When he tired of talking about himself, he asked James what he was hauling.

James decided to have some fun with him. "Dynamite," he said matter-of-factly.

"Dynamite!" the man screamed.

James told him not to worry and began to tell him about the whole procedure that was explained to him just hours before. "So you see, friend," he said to him. "There can be no explosion without a detonator."

The man was relieved. He let out a huge sigh and looked out the window. Then he turned back to face James.

"So where do you keep the detonators?' he asked innocently.

James looked him square in the eye, then glanced down at his lap, and again, very matter-of-factly, told him he was holding them.

"Are you kidding me?" McNulty screeched. "He must have shit his pants!"

"I don't know about that," James mused, "but he made me pull over right then and there, and he walked the rest of the way."

They all laughed again.

"Not bad, McCleary," Azzaro conceded.

The nights were worse. Although the afternoon hours dragged, the tiny rays of sunlight that managed to squeeze through the cracks in the rafters were comforting. But as the day pressed on, and the sun sank beneath the hilltops, darkness fell upon them.

After all of the laughing, they split up, talked quietly in pairs or tiny groups. On nights like these, soldiers of steel became much less manly and far more maudlin. They shared intimate stories about their girlfriends. They reminisced about childhood friends and the neighborhoods where they grew up. They compared the plans they once held for the future. And they all wondered silently if they were prepared to die.

James and Leo sat together, and talked in hushed tones. "What are you gonna do if we get out of here, McCleary," Leo asked.

"That's easy," he said. "I'm gonna take Maddie out for a nice dinner, probably a steak from McKluskey's, and then I'm gonna take her down to the boardwalk, find that little spot where we always sit, just underneath the pier, and I'm gonna ask her to marry me." Just saying it made him feel better for the moment.

"What about you, Leo?" he asked.

"Well, I don't have the plan that you do," he said. "But I tell you what. I'm gonna head down to the little saloon that's about five miles from my house, and I'm gonna sit there, and I'm gonna have as many shots of whiskey as it takes before I think of one."

James chuckled. "Sounds to me like you already have one."

The night limped toward morning. The hours were interminable. It was so easy, in the blackness of their prison, to consider giving up.

Hope, however, can spring sometimes from the most unlikely sources. In the corner of the room, usually huddled, was Jerry Turner, the company introvert and bona fide eccentric. He had transferred in only a few months prior. Nobody except James really knew anything about him.

In his brief time with the company, he had become a novelty. They all found him intriguing. He was small and wormy. He looked like he should be working in a laboratory, playing with white mice or mixing chemicals in test tubes. He had an enormous forehead, and his eyes, green and glassy, were set just a little too close together. Pearson said he looked like a grasshopper. He was quiet, and when he did talk, he used strange words, like *epeirogenesis* and *hexadecimal.* He did strange things too. He wore his helmet backward and saved blades of grass from every town they visited. When he began to collect the grease drippings that they all scraped off their sawdust bread each day, no one was surprised. But in such tight quarters, some of the guys started to become irritated by his weirdness. They started to ask what was wrong with him.

"How should I know, Pearson," Leo complained. "Ask McCleary. He knows something."

James knew a little something about "Crazy Jerry." Swinton

had mentioned something to him once during one of his lectures about field conduct.

While on scouting patrol in a German town that had been shelled by mortars, an entire company of soldiers, including Jerry, stumbled on a group of dead Germans. Many of the guys in Jerry's outfit stopped to pick up ammo and other items they could use.

"Now Crazy Jerry," Swinton told him, "noticed a real fancy ring with the Nazi insignia on the finger of one of the dead German officers. Others were stuffing their packs with Lugers, knives, canteens, but not Jerry. Jerry knelt down beside the dead kraut and, while singing some lines from a German lullaby one of the locals taught him, he proceeded to lift the damn ring." James was confused and a little disappointed the first time he heard the story.

"So what, Pete," he replied. "What's so crazy about that?"

"Nothing, I guess," Swinton continued, "except that the crazy bastard didn't only take the ring from the kraut; he took the goddamned finger it was on as well."

"Does he still have it, McCleary," Twitch wanted to know after James had told all of them the story.

"I don't know," James said. "Why don't you go and ask him."

They had been prisoners for five weeks. And for five weeks, they had all scraped the fatty spread off the sawdust bread they were given each morning.

Jerry had collected all of it and saved it in a can, which, they considered, wasn't all that unusual for a guy who walked around with a ring finger in his pocket.

"He's a crazy bastard all right," Azzaro remarked. "But he sure is funny."

Funny, that is, until the moment when Jerry Turner emerged as something more than just the company buffoon.

He came to them on that gloomy February night. He stood before them, silent. He was holding something behind his back. Before any of them could ask, he presented them with a candle made from weeks of grease drippings he had collected.

They were dumbfounded. Speechless. There *was* method in the madness. Who knew?

As he lifted the tiny strip of cloth wedged in the center of the fatty heap and ignited it with the matches he kept in his boots, their spirits danced with vigor and vitality. Jerry Turner's makeshift candle illuminated the entire room.

For the first time in five weeks, there were smiles. They were still prisoners, but they were not defeated. For a brief moment, they had beaten an enemy far more powerful than the Germans. For one night, they were winners.

★

John's mouth is dry again. He takes a swallow of soda and puts the postcard down on the pile of letters. He pulls out his cell phone and begins to dial home. He stops suddenly when he sees his old Yankee cap sitting on top of a pile of some moth-eaten sweaters. He puts it on. Still fits.

He is remembering his tenth birthday, when they all went to Yankee Stadium to see the Yankees play the Tigers.

He had been asking to go for a few years; James refused to take him. There always seemed to be an excuse. That's why he was so surprised when Madeline told him the good news.

It was an overcast July afternoon. John and his brothers were wearing navy and white caps and their baseball gloves. They were sitting down the right-field line, about ten rows off the field. They could smell the grass and hear some of the playful banter among the players. They had never been so close before. They pounded their gloves, hoping to catch a foul ball. So far, they hadn't even come close, but they were all smiles. James bought all of them hot dogs, and the Yanks had just pulled ahead of the Tigers on a fifth-inning home run, a powerful blast into the upper deck by their hero, Mickey Mantle: Yanks 5, Tigers 4.

Without warning, the skies over the Bronx opened up, sending a sellout crowd running for cover. Thousands of disappointed spectators spilled out of the gates and into the waiting areas outside the concession stands. There was very little room to move.

John was standing next to his father, frowning. "Daddy, is the game going to be canceled?"

James did not answer. He couldn't hear anything over the claps of thunder that exploded like mortar shells and the rain that pounded the stadium overhangs like the marching feet of German guards.

The sounds of past and present swirled together. James turned pale. A thin line of perspiration formed just above his upper lip. He grabbed for Madeline. His legs grew weak. The next minute, he was on one knee, holding his head.

"Come on, boys," she told them. "We're leaving."

"What do you mean we're leaving?" John cried.

"We are leaving. Your father isn't feeling well."

"It's gonna stop raining. We don't have to leave," he protested.

"Jonathan McCleary," Madeline reprimanded, "we are leav-ing. Now!"

"But the game is not over!" he screamed.

"You heard what I said. We are leaving. Let's go."

"But it's my birthday!"

THIRTEEN

*

James and McNulty developed high fevers. McNulty was sure they had been poisoned and that the end was near. James did all he could to quell his hysteria. He had all but convinced him that everything was okay when the orderlies came for them and took them to a building in Koblenz that doubled as a German hospital and confinement camp. They never got to say good-bye to the others.

The atmosphere at the hospital was not as austere as that of the other German camp, but they were prisoners again nonetheless. The building reminded James of the warehouse they had used once as an outpost. The outside was gray and melancholy. The stone front had been stained by fire and soot.

Two large windows way up top looked like eyes, sad and desperate. The glass had been shattered in both, and the jagged remnants gave the impression of tears suspended on gloomy lids.

The inside was fairly clean. James was assigned to a bed that stood unsteadily on a broom-swept floor. The walls were bright and solid, although he noticed several faults that looked like vines running from the ceiling right down to the floor. He wondered how safe he really was.

The room he and McNulty were given had a window; he was grateful for that. Outside, he could see the sun, warm and inviting. Chimneys were visible above trees that lined a country crossroad. It made him smile, feel normal again, although after a while, it just became another painful reminder of what he was missing.

He felt lousy. He was sweaty and hungry. His head hurt. He was out of his mind with worry. He and McNulty were uncertain where they were, but they had each other. This helped them both, especially McNulty.

"Hey, Jimmy," he whispered, afraid of the German guards standing just outside the door. "What do you figure they'll do with us now?"

"How the hell should I know, Twitch?" he answered.

James liked McNulty. He did. But it was more pity than true affection. He had spent enough time with him to know that he was a real worrier, the proverbial stick-in-the-mud. He was the kind of guy who just expected something bad to happen. He often wandered the barracks with a pen and paper in hand, revising the letter back home he had written in anticipation of his tragic demise.

"Hey, Twitch?" they always teased. "You going somewhere?"

James would have liked to have answered McNulty's question. The truth was, he didn't know how. He was feeling a little too sick to worry too much, and the nurse in charge, Schwesta Inga, had captured his attention.

She was an enigma, a German nurse in charge of POWs who behaved as if she herself was incarcerated. She was very young and nervous. Her sandy blonde hair cascaded over her shoulders, framing the contours of her face and belying the severity of her expression. Each time she entered the room, carrying food or water or medical dressings, her hands trembled so violently that by the time she had completed her rounds, more than half of the items on her tray were resting comfortably on the floor.

The Russian POW lying in the bed to his right intrigued him as well. His name was Boris. His leg had been torn apart by a German machine gunner after his entire platoon was ambushed by an enemy scouting patrol. He was the only one from his outfit who survived.

James formed a fast friendship with the Russian. He was tired of listening to Twitch and his paranoia; Boris was a welcome diversion.

Boris explained to James that Inga was dreadfully afraid of the Americans. "They are the enemy," he told him. "Animals and murderers, men to be feared." She believed all that she was told by the Nazi regime about the American soldier. When she recalled all of the death and destruction she had witnessed in her young life, how could she think otherwise?

"Victim of too many air raids," Boris continued.

Now several of them, including himself and McNulty, were thrust upon her. She was so paralyzed with fear that she could barely look at them.

"Well, how does she feel about you, comrade?" James asked sheepishly. Boris laughed.

"About me?" he replied. "She like me. Feel sorry for me. Russian Jew in Nazi hospital not such good thing."

Boris discussed the plight of most Russian soldiers who were injured and brought to these German hospitals. "Depending on severity of injury," he explained, "Russian prisoner has three possibilities: amputation, experimentation, or elimination." He was looking at his own leg the entire time.

"Boris just waiting," he added glibly.

"Why don't you do something?" James implored. "How can you just sit there?"

Boris's face never changed expression. "What's to do?" he replied. "I am Jew; they are Nazis. Boris can't change that."

James thought about how lucky he had been. It was certainly one of his flaws, measuring himself against others. It hardly seemed fair. Why had he been spared so many times? Why didn't this good fortune extend to others, like Sully, Erikson, and Hinson? And to Boris? What was it that made him impervious to the tragedy that had befallen so many others?

The miraculous medal. Could it have been as simple as that? Could this tiny piece of polished alloy be the force that served and protected him? He recalled the day his mother gave it to him. A little white box with two shiny medals inside.

"There are two, sweetheart, in case something happens," she explained. He kissed her cheek and thanked her. She smiled. "She will guide you, Jimmy. Just believe."

He wondered if his mom really had known, especially in light of all of the close calls he had had: an errant grenade that fell into his bunker, killing the man to his left and taking the arm of the one to his right; an old brick church that was ground to dust by a mortar just moments after he had left; a miraculous jaunt across an embankment they later named Suicide Ridge. It was easy to find God on the battlefield.

✱

Schwesta Inga slipped into their room one morning to complete the provisions for Boris's move. Just before she wheeled him away, James called out. "Stop," he said, waving his hands frantically. He removed the medal from around his neck and handed it to the Russian. "You are a good Catholic, Boris," James told him, speaking loud enough for the entire room to hear. They both smiled. "Don't worry, comrade," he whispered, as Inga wheeled him away. "She will guide you."

Across the way from the hospital building where James and the other injured prisoners were kept was a German kitchen where the healthy POWs went at the end of the day to get their tiny bowls filled with soup. Most were permitted only three or four trips a week. The Russian prisoners, however, were allowed to go to the line just once every seven days. A single ladle of soup and an occasional slice of stale bread was all they were given for the week.

James noticed that many of these Russian prisoners were just like Boris. They were kind men with soft, sad eyes. After Boris was taken away, James was riddled with grief. He wandered from his building into the kitchen area hoping to learn the whereabouts of his foreign comrade. The modest metal soup bowl he lifted off a cart was his passport from his room at the hospital into the kitchen on days when only the Russians and a handful of other healthy prisoners were to receive their soup.

James was sickened by the number of starving Russian prisoners lined up like dogs, waiting for their meager serving of po-
tato soup. They were dirty. He could scarcely see the tear streaks
and frown lines beneath their grimy cheeks. The smell of sweat
and fear was strong, like spoiled fruit or turpentine. Their dark,
drawn faces and emaciated frames were painful snapshots of a
world he no longer recognized. Still, he kept going back, be-
lieving each time that it was the trip that would lead him back to
Boris.

Despite the misery and repeated failure, James continued
looking for Boris until the incident that resulted in his being
ordered away from the kitchen area permanently. James arrived
at the soup line the same way he always did: he entered quietly
through the back of the cooking area, careful to avoid the two
vicious German shepherds who served as sentinels of the
kitchen. He took his place at the end of the line. He stood
silently, running his right thumb over the cold rim of his soup
bowl, looking for Boris or anyone who might have seen him. He
noticed one of the Russians sneak off the line momentarily and
walk over to a garbage Dumpster on the left side of the line. He
continued to watch as the desperate man scanned the room before reaching into the receptacle and grabbing a fist full of po-
tato skins, which he then stuffed under his coat before
returning to the line.

Moments later, a young German guard approached the fidg-
ety Russian. "Empty coat," he ordered, extending his cold hand
to the prisoner. The Russian ignored the request. "Empty coat,"
he repeated. Still no response from the Russian. "Empty coat
now," he said again, removing a Luger from his belt. The Russian just stared into his eyes.

Frustrated and fearful of an insurrection, the guard fired a single shot into the chest of the stubborn prisoner, killing him instantly. He glared at the others before walking back to his post.

The minute he turned his back, another Russian walked over to the corpse and took the skins. The guard saw this and shot the second man immediately. Each time the guard turned away, another Russian approached the victim and with grim determination took the skins, only to suffer a similar fate. After the fourth prisoner was killed, several guards who had become alarmed by the commotion came rushing in to investigate, and the incident was over.

James tried to exit as surreptitiously as he had entered, but the presence of the other guards thwarted his efforts.

"You, Ami," one of the older guards called to him. "Come here."

James walked slowly in the direction of the request.

"What are you doing with Russians? Does Ami boy want to die like Russian?" he asked, jamming his pistol into James's ribs.

James looked into his eyes but said nothing.

"Now go away," the German demanded, "and forget what you see."

James returned to the hospital building, his head reeling. He vomited in his bowl several times before settling back in his bed. "Forget what you see," he repeated to himself. If only he could.

He felt strange. Maybe it was the absence of the medal. He wished he had the other one with him. Maybe it was just the cumulative effect of all of the pain and suffering he had seen. He wasn't certain.

Even Schwesta Inga seemed different. He noticed, for instance, that her hands had stopped shaking. She was calm and did not turn her head when her eyes met his. He would have spent more time considering the possibilities if he had not been so concerned with Boris.

He wondered if he had made the right decision. Maybe the Nazis would have overlooked the fact that Boris was a Jew. He should have kept the medal. What if it actually made them more suspicious? Or angry? What if they came looking for its rightful owner? Everything was out of joint. The only thing that remained the same was the neurotic, irritating voice of Twitch.

"Hey, Jimmy," he called from across the room. "What do you suppose happened to the Russian?"

James sighed.

*

He was awakened early the next morning by the sound of Inga preparing the bed to his right.

Replacement for Boris, he thought to himself. He was not surprised. It had been weeks since James had seen him.

When Inga was just about finished preparing the bed, she turned to James. She placed her hand into the front pocket of her apron and removed a bar of chocolate that one of the German officers had given to her. She broke it and handed him half. She smiled.

"Must get bed ready, Ami," she said. "Catholic boy will be back soon." She smiled again. Then, as she tucked the fourth and final corner of the bed sheet under the mattress, Schwesta

Inga gave James McCleary the cutest little wink he had ever seen.

Boris returned. He looked pale, but when he saw James, a smile swept across his face. He pointed to his leg and smirked. "Good as new," he said.

James smiled. "How did everything go?" he asked. "Any problems?"

"None. You were right. It's very good luck."

James's consciousness seemed to split. He was thinking of his mother, how she would love this story.

"Do you want medal back, James?" Boris asked tentatively, touching his hand to his chest.

"No, Boris," he replied. "You keep it."

The Russian sighed and leaned back in his bed. "I was hoping you say that."

It wasn't long before they were on the move once again. German intelligence had issued the deflating news that the Americans were inching closer to the facility; orders to move the entire camp farther back into Germany soon followed.

So under a dark winter sky, the German guards loaded the wounded into a boxcar at the rear of a railroad train. The rattletrap car was packed from wall to wall with bodies. James continued to look for Boris. McNulty managed to find a place on the cold wood floor right next to James. The two of them did not budge all night as the rickety train moaned and groaned through the countryside en route to a destination somewhere in the bowels of Germany.

The sun climbed over the frosty hills that morning just the way it did every day. But on this particular morning, it failed to extend its arms into the crowded boxcar. They remained in darkness for many hours. All of the prisoners soon realized the train was stuck in a cold, dark tunnel the Germans were using to shield them from American planes circling above.

"I can't believe I'm saying this, McCleary," McNulty stammered, "but I'm sure glad we're stuck in here." He rubbed his chewed fingers together feverishly and raised them to his mouth, blowing short blasts of breath in the space between his thumbs. "Can you imagine coming all this way," he continued. "The hill, the hospital, this godforsaken trip in this broken-down piece of shit only to be destroyed by our own aircraft? No thank you! Not me. I'm staying right here."

They languished in the tunnel for thirty-six hours during which they were given no food or water. Toward the end of the second day, James and the others heard from one of the German guards in another car that there were peasants, some of them French, in the tunnel, asking for a glimpse of the American prisoners on board.

"Come, Amis," he announced. "We will show you the dirt you wish to die for."

The wounded Americans gathered around as the German slid the rusty metal door open. Light crept into the tunnel from the opening, exposing a group of civilians. They were screaming and crying, waving their hands with what looked to be violent disapproval. Some extended their hands into the white drifts that still lined the openings of the tunnel and began pelting the train with balls fashioned from the remaining snow.

The German guard, bored by the endless hours he had spent on the train, was amused. He laughed at the startled Americans.

"What the hell are they doing?" McNulty screamed in disgust. The others were baffled as well. "Hey!" McNulty screamed in protest. "Hey, you stupid, ungrateful bastards! We're here for *you!*"

The balls of snow just kept coming. It wasn't until James noticed one of the Russian prisoners on board pick up one of the snowballs and place it in his mouth that he realized what was happening. The anger was not directed at them. The snow was not an instrument of attack. It was a gift of life, given to them by simple allies who recognized the gravity of their situation.

The snowballs proved to be a harbinger of better things. When the train arrived at the new facility, a dark, menacing structure encircled by a rusty barbed wire fence, they were all surprised to find that most of the Germans who had been assigned to guard the camp had left. As they were ushered into the facility and led through a courtyard overrun with what looked like dead cucumber vines, they couldn't help but infer some meaning from all the empty chairs stationed at each post. James had not expected to feel this way, like perhaps things were finally changing.

They did. Two weeks later, all of them awoke to find that the rest of the German guards had left, dropped everything, and fled.

Many of the incarcerated men, overwhelmed by the rush of relief and residue of anger, began running through the camp, firing guns and words of hate and destroying the walls. James saw one of the Russians, a tall, skinny man with piercing eyes, dragging two German Shepherds around by their tails, as his comrades laughed and cheered.

The Free French Interior was sweeping through France and

into Germany, accompanied by American troops, liberating the prison camps and hospitals. The image of the tall skinny Russian and the dogs bothered him. But the sight of friendly uniforms was, for James, the happiest moment of the war.

FOURTEEN

✯

Okay, Mr. McCleary. I'll just need your father's signature on this release, and a copy of the key, and I can start showing the house."

"That shouldn't be a problem, Lucy," John says, holding his hand out to meet hers. "I am eager—and so is my father, of course—to finalize everything. We've been cleaning like crazy here."

"I see that. I noticed all the bags by the curb when I pulled up. Looks like a lot of years were spent here."

Her words send a chill up his back, like fingernails on a chalkboard. He scans the pile through the window. Grandma McCleary's crib; the door jamb; bags of old clothes, books, and toys. He feels bad. It is of little consequence, he concludes. In another day or two, it will be as if none of it ever even existed.

"Well, you know the old expression," he says to her cavalierly. "To every thing, there is a season."

John shuts the door behind him. He walks to the kitchen for some water. His eyes wander to the hand-carved sign that still sits above the sink: THE MCCLEARYS. He fills a glass and gazes out the window.

The leaves have just begun to fall from the trees. A squirrel is crossing the lawn, busy with the chores of the season. The high-beams from the neighbor's car burn through a light fog, giving everything he sees a dreamlike quality.

His stomach hurts. He has not eaten yet. He considers running down to the deli on the corner, but there is still work to be done.

James has just sat down. He pulls a newspaper from a wicker basket jammed with curling paperbacks and crossword puzzles. John moves deliberately in his direction. "Here," he says, dropping the contract in his lap. "You need to sign this."

Soon he is back upstairs, holding James's pack. He continues to look through it, searching for another glimpse into a life he has only just discovered. He unzips a pouch. More letters. In another he finds a pair of socks and a small, brown envelope. He opens it. Inside is a silver chain with a religious medal. His eyes fill with tears. He has seen it before.

He is chilled by the discovery. He feels an urgency, a painful longing to tell someone about what he has just pieced together. But it is only a little past noon. Matt and Paul will not be by for several hours. He cannot wait that long. He is halfway down the stairs when he looks over at the chair by the window; James is asleep.

Frustrated, he goes back to the attic. He tries to finish packing the items that remain but is far too restive for such work. He takes out his cell phone and scrolls through the menu, looking for his wife's number at work.

"When are you coming home, John?" she asks him.

"The day after tomorrow. I hope," he says, looking at the work that still needs to be done. "The house should be empty by tomorrow. Listen, I—"

"J.R. told me he called you with his good news. What do you think?"

"I don't know," he says. He is fingering the silver chain while she speaks.

"Hard to believe," she says. "Our little boy . . . a United States Marine."

"Yeah. He sounded pretty excited," John says. "But I—"

"Oh, he is," she tells him. There is a pause. "So how is everything going there?"

"That's why I'm calling," he tells her. "I have learned some interesting things these past few days. And I just discovered something that is really unbelievable."

He begins to tell her about the international electronics convention he attended in London a few years back. And the man who approached him that first night. John felt his gaze, the way the stranger followed his every movement, as if reading a chapter in a mystery. He was tempted to approach him, to ask why he was staring, but the stranger beat him to it.

He was tall and thin. His face was pale and dotted with what looked like the beginnings of a beard. His suit hung loosely on his frame. He reminded John of a character he had seen once in an old Jimmy Stewart movie.

"Excuse me, sir," said the voice. "I couldn't help noticing your name tag. Are you from New York?"

"No, California," John answered.

There is obvious disappointment on the face of the stranger. "Well, do you have relatives in New York?" the man asked.

"Actually, I'm originally from there," John answered. "I grew up in Rockaway Beach."

The stranger smiled. "Andrei Vyacheslav," he said, extending his hand.

"John McCleary. Nice to meet you."

They talked briefly about their companies and the itinerary for the weekend. John grew tired quickly and excused himself.

"Okay," Andrei said. "But can I ask you just one more question?"

"Sure," he said.

"I hope you don't mind, but was your father in the war?" he asked.

"Yes."

"My father was too. The Russian army," Andrei explained.

"Interesting," John replied.

"My father always talked about a man he met," Andrei explained. "From New York. His name was James McCleary."

John looked at him quizzically. "That's funny," he said. "That's my father's name. But it's not that uncommon. I'm sure there are plenty of James McClearys in New York."

John clicked his briefcase closed. He stood up and pushed in his chair. "Excuse me, Andrei," he said, looking at his watch. "I really have to go." He gave a gratuitous smile and walked away.

"He wasn't a POW, was he?" Andrei persisted, calling after him.

John turned and crept back, slowly. "Yes, I think he was," he said uncomfortably. "But he never spoke about it."

Tiny beads of sweat formed between the lines on John's forehead. He stood in silence, as if waiting for the matter to conclude on its own volition, until Andrei spoke again. "If you have a little time, I think I have something I should share with you."

Andrei began telling John all about his father, Boris. He started by explaining how he valued his friendship with this American more than anything. "He said they talked about everything, John," Andrei explained. "Shared a hospital room."

John nodded.

"And there's more," Andrei said. "This American? Your father? He saved *my* father's life. While they were in that German hospital. Helped him survive. But he never got . . . he never got the chance to thank him."

Andrei wiped his eyes. "It always bothered him."

John was considering the chimerical implication of Andrei's suggestion. "That is certainly an unbelievable story, Andrei," John said. "Really. But I have to tell you. The man you are describing does not sound like my father."

Andrei loosened his tie and opened the top two buttons on his shirt. John was puzzled. He watched as the man reached his fingers inside and pulled out a silver chain, with a religious medal. "This is what this man gave to my father," he said with difficulty. "I have worn it every day since he passed. The man who saved my father wore the same one. It's the Blessed Mother. Do you recognize it?"

John shook his head. "I'm sorry, Andrei," John said. "But my father does not have one of those."

The Russian man's face dropped. "Okay. I just thought I'd ask," he said dejectedly. "But if at some time you should find out that it was your father," he continued, handing him a business card, "please call me."

John continues to detail for his wife the encounter with the Russian stranger. "Are you kidding me?" she says. "That's amazing. Do you think it's possible? Is that possible?"

He turns the medal between his thumb and index finger. "I'm not sure, Michele," he says. "I'm just not sure."

"Well, either way, it sounds like your time there has been good for you," she says. "Maybe you should discuss it with Dr. Canfield. Let him know what you're thinking."

There is a protracted silence on his end.

"You do remember we have an appointment this Saturday, right, John?"

"Yeah, yeah. I remember."

"Because you cannot miss another one. You know that, John, right?"

"No, I'll be there," he tells her. "I'm landing Friday night."

★

Marriage counseling. It was Michele's idea. The last attempt at repairing a relationship that had slowly buckled beneath the weight of what Canfield called *latent, unresolved tensions.*

"What the fuck does that mean, Michele!" he exploded in

the car on the way home from his office after their first meeting. "This is your answer to our problems?"

Labels and rhetoric. God, how he hated the rhetoric. Psychobabble he called it. It was useless. All he knew was that there were things in his house that he did not like. Things that made him angry and tense. And now some self-appointed expert on the dynamics of marital intercourse wanted to label him, lay the blame right at his feet.

"I'm not crazy, Michele," he told her. "I know crazy. I lived with it my whole life."

When they were first married, everything was wonderful, fresh and alive. She traveled with him overseas on business. They enjoyed long, intimate exchanges on the rocks at La Jolla Cove. Many nights they dined al fresco down in Balboa Park at Prado's or delighted in surprise bubble baths and hot fudge sundaes at one-thirty in the morning. And sex. God, the sex was unreal. They behaved most often like teenagers, tearing at each other, anywhere, anytime. He remembered how she used to come to him, her head tilted slightly to the side, a girlish look in her eyes, almost embarrassed that he knew exactly what she was thinking.

Then the kids came. And this spontaneous, willful girl withdrew, became an alien presence. He scarcely knew her anymore. He spent most of his time groping for the past, struggling to resurrect their moribund relationship. It always ended in arguments. He complained that she was different. She insisted he was insensitive and controlling. He yelled a lot too, at her and the kids. She wasn't totally wrong about him. Did he want control? Sure. When things start slipping away from you, who doesn't want to reach out and pull them back? He continued to yell. They rarely went out together. Talk was all too often limited to the kids, and sex was reduced to an occasional encounter sandwiched between arguments and weeks of masturbatory substitutes.

He was content to weather the storm. Michele had other ideas. After years of contention, she thought it was time they sought counseling. Dr. Canfield was going to save their marriage. They were making some progress. They figured out they still loved each other and that they both wanted this to work, but then Madeline got sick, and John's attention shifted from one problem to another.

FIFTEEN

✯

Toward the end of the conflict in Europe, thousands of American trucks, Jeeps, tanks, and personnel carriers rumbled through the towns of Germany, accompanied by a halo of B-17s and B-24s. The infantry flooded the interior of the land, pouring over the countryside with strength and numbers that the Germans had underestimated.

The sun had ascended to the highest point in the brilliant blue sky. The smell of flowers, just in bloom, floated on warm, soothing breezes. They were at rest, about three miles from the front, enjoying a little down time.

James, Leo, and Pearson were smoking and playing cards

when they heard the news. Patrick McNulty told them. He was stuttering and crying. He could barely get the words out.

"What the hell is wrong *now,* Twitch?" Pearson asked.

"The krauts," he said. "They're gone. Swinton and the colonel. Said they fell on the Russian line. Something about being outmanned. We're home! Ah, ha ha. Home! Can you believe it? We're going home!"

The reaction of the others was guarded. They had been disappointed before.

"You better not be shittin' us, McNulty," Pearson warned.

"Shut up, Pearson," Leo interrupted. "Let him catch his breath."

McNulty sat down next to James and took a swallow from Leo's canteen. "I'm telling you guys," he continued. "I heard Swinton talking to the colonel. It's true. It's all but over, fellas. The fat lady is singing! I think they said Eisenhower is going to make the announcement sometime today."

Hours later, McNulty's news was confirmed. The others joined the celebration. They had waited a long time. Now it was here. Finally here. At camp, they drank heavily and entertained themselves with cards, letter writing, and fantastic tales of what they would be doing back in the states.

"When I get home, I'm going straight to Alonso's," Azzaro declared, "and get me some pretty little pastry."

"Hey, Schnozzola," Pearson teased. "What makes you think she's still interested? I bet a lot of other guys got little notes in their rolls while you were gone."

The others laughed. Even Azzaro smiled. He couldn't be mad. Not today.

They continued to celebrate, but they weren't leaving just

yet. There was still work to be done. The German soldiers were still around. And the threat of violence remained. It would be a while before they were deployed back to the States. And for some, who had not earned the eighty-five service points needed for a discharge, they would have to make a stop in the land of the rising sun before returning home. In the meantime, the victors would have many intimate encounters with German civilians determined to repair the fragments of their shattered lives.

James and Leo were fortunate. Many of their comrades were forced to reside in blown-out factories or small, dilapidated houses. Not them. They found themselves sharing a large German house with a family of five. It was good living.

Each evening, after having spent the better part of the day patrolling the littered streets of Lechbruck, playing the role of military police to the defeated Germans, they came together with their German hosts to share food and drink and conversation about the recent events that had thrown them all together.

The house was in exceptionally good condition, particularly in light of the shelling that had all but decimated virtually every other building within miles: flowered curtains on the windows; rose satin wallpaper trimmed with handcrafted oak moldings; a long, downy sofa, adorned with crocheted afghans and several rectangular throw pillows. And when Pearson heard about the beautiful cherry wood piano, he tried everything he could to weasel his way inside.

"Forget it, Pearson," James warned. "There's no more room."

"Come on," he complained. "One song. Just one song."

James enjoyed talking with the elderly gentleman who lived there with his daughter and her family. He was simple. An old man with graying temples and a maroon wool sweater. He had a broken smile, but the light in his eyes still flickered with hope.

It was Sunday morning. The family turned the kitchen over to them so they could prepare breakfast: fresh eggs and a warm loaf of raisin bread, given to them by the old man.

"How do you want them today, McCleary?" Leo asked, banging an egg on the rim of a mixing bowl.

"How about without shells this time?" he joked.

After breakfast, James sat on a wicker trunk, sipping the wine he and Leo looted from one of the other homes. He listened to the old German and was moved by his humanity.

"I never trust him," he said. "That Hitler." Like so many of the older German civilians they had spoken to, he hated the Nazi war machine. "We thank God for Americans," he continued. He reached under his shirt and kissed the crucifix that hung from his neck. "Americans," he said with a faint smile, "do God's work."

James wasn't so sure he agreed, but they continued, nonetheless, with their efforts to restore order to the beleaguered town. There was much to be done and very little time.

The tiny town was in a shambles. Buildings were crumbling; streets and sidewalks were littered with debris; civilians wept while rummaging through piles of rubble, trying to salvage what little was left of a time since past. James and the others looked everywhere for a sign, something to assure them that they had indeed been victorious; all they could see was the bitter face of inhumanity staring back at them.

On one corner, James and Leo met a man with a dirty face, no shirt, and tattered trousers. He was playing an accordion, "Der Lindenbaum," an old German folk song. The music was shrill and echoed in and out of the holes in the vacant stone dwellings and across the shattered rooftops that were dozing under a quiet sky. The man squeezed his arms together with conviction and pressed the keys hard. His eyes were shut tight, so tight they appeared to be two slits just wide enough to release tears that dropped off his cheeks, one after the other. They listened for as long as they could, then moved on. Each day brought more of the same.

Six weeks later, James received the official word: he was going home. He sat with Leo. Despite the joy of the moment, everything appeared to him to be unutterably sad. Neither one of them really knew what to say. Maybe it was the smell of civilization, a smell he no longer recognized. Maybe he was just so damn used to the army, he couldn't fathom anything else. He pushed his thumb and forefinger to the bridge of his nose. He rubbed his eyes. Then he finally spoke. "Call me sometime, Leonardo. Okay?"

"Yeah, McCleary. You bet."

The next day, with a pocket full of addresses and a pair of socks tucked securely under his right arm, Corporal James Mc-Cleary set his sights on Rockaway Beach—and Madeline.

★

When James returned home, the first thing he did was climb into a hot shower. He stood there for almost an hour, while the warm water splashed across his back and neck, unleashing a storm of images. Each one bounced off the corners of his memory like a tiny rubber ball.

Now that he was home, it felt as though it had never happened at all. Like maybe it was just a book he had finished or a movie he had seen. There was a comfortable detachment. Standing there, he thought he could easily be sitting at the Park Theater, watching as each frame of film dissolved into the next. The scenes were certainly familiar, but the man on screen was a stranger.

Who is this guy? he thought to himself. It was surreal. He was ducking shells and mortars one minute and on a boat back to the states the next. It all happened so fast.

He couldn't wait to see Madeline. He delighted in the joy of rediscovering her. When they were together, he was alive again. His body tingled. He continued to feel things that he never had before. The blood moving under his skin, the tiny hairs on his arms and on the back of his neck, every blink of his eyes.

"God, I missed sitting here with you, Maddie," he told her that evening, as the two of them looked out at the water from their sandy seats.

"I did too, Jimmy," she whispered.

He was looking into her eyes, soft and green, sparkling with tiny flecks of grey and yellow. He took his finger and gently pushed the hair away from her temples, tucking the errant strands neatly behind her ears. With the same finger, he traced the contours of her face. "I love you, Maddie," he said tenderly.

The two lovers lost themselves in a swoon of passion. The sun, slipping below the watery horizon, caught the broken clouds, creating a glowing yellow that seemed to bathe their bodies in heavenly approval. Her lips were soft and warm, like rose petals soaked in the afternoon sun. The sensation of her hands on his back and the brush of her lashes against his cheek, like the wistful dance of butterfly wings, were exhilarating. His tongue danced over her lips and across her teeth. After a few seconds of exploration, it found hers, a playful dance that ignited a passion that spread to his hands, sending his fingers dancing across her shuddering body. When the exchange became too intense for public view, they skipped across the pier and found a private spot under the boardwalk, a place where their bodies were free to move together, a rhythmic rising and falling, like the undulating waves behind them.

Being with her was as effortless as breathing in the salty Rockaway air. They spent many days walking the shore, talking about the possibilities that lay before them and anything else that happened to pop into their heads, laughing each time the frothy surf licked their feet. Madeline marveled at the collection of kites that scraped the sky high above their heads. "They look just like spaceships or maybe mythological creatures," she giggled. He loved how everything she saw turned into an idea. So often her thoughts filled the space in his head until he was lost, wonderfully lost, in the worlds she created.

Rockaway Beach welcomed home all of her sons with a pomp and circumstance unlike anything the tiny town had seen before. There was a parade or gathering on every street. Businesses opened their doors to the young heroes, honoring them with complimentary food and drink and anything else they could ever need or want. They were the talk of the town.

James was overwhelmed by this status he suddenly possessed. He couldn't go anywhere without a fuss. He wasn't on Main Street more than ten minutes when a woman pushing a baby carriage and holding the hand of her other child stopped him and Madeline. "Thank you," she said, kissing his cheek before throwing her arms around his neck.

Madeline looked on.

"You are so wonderful, really," the woman continued. "It's so good that you're home. We all missed you. Isn't that right, Tommy," she said to the little boy at her side.

He broke away from his mother and wrapped his tiny arms as far as they would go around James's leg. "You're a real hero," she said, before continuing on her way.

James blushed. Madeline smiled.

"That was really nice," she said to him. "Who was that?"

James scratched his head. "I have no idea."

There were also house parties, impromptu gatherings that stretched for blocks, electrifying the tiny town of Rockaway until all hours of the night. Between the intimate moments with Madeline and his family, James found himself the guest of honor at many celebrations. For sixty-one consecutive days, James, Pete Riley, T. J. McMullan, Johnny Santoras, and every other town hero was swept away in a whirlwind of music, dancing, and drinking that appeared to have no end. Each night was at a different house.

"It's good to be home, Jimmy, eh?" T.J. said, raising a glass filled with beer up in front of his face. His feet were moving to the swing music coming from the adjoining room. "And tomorrow, we can do it all over again at the Wallach's place."

"Sure is, buddy," James replied, grabbing Madeline and breaking into a full-scale jitterbug. "Who's got it better than us?"

But after sixty-one days of celebrating, Rockaway Beach slowly returned to the normal routine of day-to-day life. Somehow, this did not include its heroes. There was no place in town for a field radio operator. Nobody needed a machine gunner or tank commander. The faint sounds of music and laughter lingered in the air. But reality had crept up on all of them and slapped them hard.

The bar stools at Billie's Tavern became pulpits from which these fallen idols espoused their philosophies on life after war. Their ideas were as varied as their experiences.

"Did you hear what happened to me at Stegner's, T.J.?" James asked

"No, McCleary. What are you talking about?"

"I went down to Stegner's to get some chicken for my mom," he explained. "I had a little run in with the new butcher who's helping old man Stegner."

"You mean Scott Sanders?" T.J. said.

"I don't know his name," James replied.

"Red hair? Bum foot?"

"Yeah," James said. "That's it. You know him?"

"No, not really," T.J. said. "His mom and my mom are friendly. She told me he's working there."

"Well, he's lucky I didn't take his goddamned head off."

"Why?" T.J. asked. "What the hell happened?"

"He was just a prick, that's all."

"Well, he must have done something to get you," T.J. persisted.

"Ah, I don't know."

T.J. finished his beer and ordered another.

"Can I ask you a stupid question?" James said.

T.J. laughed. "Sure, Jimmy. It's not like it's never happened before."

"Rockaway Beach, this neighborhood, the people— everything looks the same. You know. Like before we left. But it all seems so weird. Different. Do you know what I mean?"

"Yeah, Jimmy," he said, wiping the corners of his mouth with his fingers. "I know."

★

James did a lot of thinking, but very little of it was about the future. He thought a lot about Inga. He never had the chance to say good-bye. Or thank you. She cleared out in the middle of the night with the rest of the Nazi officials. He had trouble forgetting the faces of John Sullivan and Daniel Erikson and two German boys, one with a white flag and the other a mountain jacket. He wondered if Boris made it out okay. And when he would finally receive a letter or phone call from Leo.

His mother began to lose her patience with him. She allowed him the space and time he needed to get acclimated once again to civilian life. But days turned into weeks and weeks into months, without any sign that he was ready to assume a normal existence. "What did you do today, Jimmy?" she asked him one day after returning from work.

"Nothing," he told her.

"Nothing?" she questioned.

"Well, I was down at Maddie's for a while," he explained. "I went over to T.J.'s after that. Then I came back here."

"Didn't you see Mr. Jantzen about getting your old job back?" she asked.

"No. I didn't have time to do that," he said.

The expression on her face became severe. "You didn't have time?" she repeated. "Are you kidding, James? All you have is time."

"Stop bothering me about this, Mom," he complained. "I told you. I just don't feel like it. You don't understand."

"What I understand, James, is that you need to start behaving like an adult. Enough of this. You've had your fun. Now it's time to go back to work."

Time passed. He was restless. And this restlessness kept bumping into things like his family, his friends, and the nameless future. He worried. He didn't want to drift anymore. There was little relief at home. When his mother was not badgering him to find a job and move on, his brothers were under his skin. When he looked at Thomas and Michael, all he saw was his own life, the way it could have been. "First born," he lamented. It was a raw deal. The only time that being first meant you lost. The first to lose your childhood. First to sacrifice your plans for others. First to war.

When they talked carelessly of high school baseball games, the soda shop, and plans for college, and philosophized about life itself from the safety of the cocoon he had helped build for them, a bitterness rose from deep inside his stomach.

"Hey, Jimmy. Tell us what it was like beating on the Germans," they asked.

"Nah," he said. "You guys don't want to hear about that."

It was several weeks before James started working again. Like many things, it all seemed so trivial to him: nine-to-five; twenty-minute coffee breaks; punching a time clock. In the grand scheme, what did it matter?

This disillusionment followed him to every job he attempted. There were several: the corner gas station; an apprenticeship with Mr. Langlin, the carpenter who did most of the work for many of the local businesses and residents. He even worked a couple of days at the butcher shop, accepting old man Stegner's offer as an apology for the way he had been treated that afternoon. But he could not focus.

"I can't see the purpose," he continued to tell his mother.

Madeline remained a blessing, that is, until she began to pressure him into something he was not ready to handle.

"Well, Mr. McCleary," she said to him as they walked on the damp sand of Rockaway Beach. "What do you think?"

"About what?" James replied.

She made a face. "Come on. Don't tease me, Jimmy. Us. What do you think about us?"

He was certain that he loved Madeline. It was the only thing he did know. It was the other expectation associated with such a commitment that he was inclined to ignore. He had it all planned before he got home, just as he told Leo: McKlutzsky's Steak House, the romantic walk down to the pier, a marriage proposal. It had seemed like a good idea. Now, for whatever reason, it didn't feel quite that way. His head was filled with so many things. He reached down to pick up a cream-colored shell whose perfection and symmetry were spoiled only by a small chip on its underside. He cast it back into the surf.

"I think you know the answer to that question, Maddie." he said.

She stopped walking and put her hands on his cheeks. "Jimmy," she said. "It's been over three months now. We lost two years already. I want to start living the life we've always spoken about. Now. I don't want to wait anymore."

"I know what you want, Maddie. I know," he told her. "I want the same thing. I do. But I . . . Well, I just need a little time . . . to figure things out."

"What is there to figure out, James?" she protested. "If you want the same thing, there *is* nothing to figure out."

One by one, his friends began resuming normal lives. Some

enrolled in college; others began careers. Many got married and started families of their own. The fear of being left behind, of remaining lost in a world that no longer existed, was enough to shake James's ambition from its slumber.

He remained unsure as to what he wanted to do, but he was tired of floundering. "I don't care what you do, James," his mother hollered, "just do something!"

He got his old position back at the A & P. Not much had changed since he left. The familiarity was a comfort of sorts, but he left several times. Just got up and walked out of the store. He didn't feel right. It wasn't the same after all. He often felt like he couldn't breathe, like someone had strapped one of those dreadful produce crates to his back and it was pushing all of the air from his lungs.

It was during these moments he thought about fighting in the hedgerows, how the massive arms of the trees on either side of the sunken roads would embrace up top, forming a leafy tunnel that suffocated the light and any hope for a safe, timely exit. It was like being suspended in a maze, a twisting, irregular labyrinth of brush and vegetation. It was hard for him to breathe.

Mr. Jantzen was patient with James. "McCleary, I'd like to talk with you after you're through with your shift," he told him.

The two of them sat in the back of the storeroom across from each other, struggling to get comfortable on a couple of empty banana crates. James liked Mr. Jantzen. He was fair and never spoke to him in the condescending tone that most people Jantzen's age used.

"What's bothering you, son?" Jantzen began. "The other day I went to look for you and someone said you were gone. Just up and left."

"I'm sorry, Mr. Jantzen," James answered. He was ashamed and embarrassed and humiliated at the thought of having disappointed his boss.

"I'll get my things," he said.

"Wait a minute, son. Hold on now. Sit back down. You'll do no such thing. That's not why I asked to see you. I asked to see you because I wanted to tell you a little story I don't tell many people."

James returned to his seat, relieved. The thought of being fired and having to tell his mother was more than he could handle at the present moment.

"I was a soldier in the First World War, James," he explained. "Did you know that?"

"No, sir," James replied. "I don't think I did."

"Yup. I was a member of the Fourth Infantry Division. Saw action in France."

James was interested but not sure where Jantzen was heading.

"Do you know it took me almost eight years before I felt even a little like myself again. Eight years! All I could think about were gas masks and trenches. I went through five jobs myself before this one. They called all of us The Lost Generation because so many of us had trouble coming back. It's not easy, James. You feel useless. Like you don't really belong. You know?"

"Yes, Mr. Jantzen," James said. "I think I know what you mean."

"Of course you do, son," he said. "It's no different. People are people. I think every generation finds its own way to get lost. It's rough. Right now your head is filled with a lot of things. But I want you to know that it's okay. People will say things to you that are gonna stick in your craw. They just won't understand.

They think they do, but they don't. You have to learn to turn a deaf ear. That's all. You'll figure it out."

Jantzen began to describe how after the war, his father told him that he would be working with him at the Machine Glass Factory, where he had worked for years. The place was dark and the air inside close. He had spent the better part of two years underground, cowering in trenches and tunnels, struggling to breathe. It was only when he returned that he realized just how much he missed the sky. Now his father wanted to shut him back inside. Young Arthur Jantzen was far too restive for this sort of thing. Working an assembly line for ten hours a day was more than he could handle.

"So one day, I'm at my post, and, I don't know, I must have been daydreaming, because before I knew it, seventeen panes of glass had slid past me. The boss complained to my father, and he blew a fit. I can still hear him screaming. Called me a bum. Then kicked me out of the warehouse. He left me sitting, out in the street. 'You don't want to work here,' he said to me, 'then find your own job.' "

After Jantzen's father chastised him, Mr. Brauer, the old man who sold produce in the little town from his fruit barrow, wandered by. He was getting too old and weak to push the wooden cart all day. He was looking for some help. Jantzen jumped at the opportunity. It was certainly better than standing inside the factory all day.

James was picking at the skin around his thumb nail. He was tired of listening. "How did that help you figure anything out?" he finally asked.

"It didn't," Jantzen said. "In fact, it made things a whole lot worse with my father. But there was this girl—brown eyes, curly hair—who used to stop by every day for apples."

Jantzen was smiling. James caught on. "Mrs. Jantzen?" James asked.

"The one and only," he replied. "After that, everything else was easy."

James and Madeline continued to spend every one of his days off together, just the way they used to. They began to talk excitedly about their plans for the future. "You know, Maddie," he told her. "I've been thinking. Maybe I could go back to school. Work during the day, college at night. I might like to be a pharmacist or a doctor. Something like that. What do you think?"

"I think that's wonderful, Jimmy," she said.

"Because I can't stay at the A & P forever. I mean, I just can't see it."

"That's okay. You don't have to explain yourself to me."

"But what about us?" he asked. "I mean, college could take a while, Maddie."

"Look, Jimmy. What you want to do is wonderful. And it's not going to be easy. But what I think is that having a lot of support—you know, a wife and maybe a family—that could really make a difference." She was smiling and batting her lashes playfully.

"Madeline Brandt," he whispered softly. "I think you are trying to tell me something."

SIXTEEN

★

Many years after the war, Chris Leonardo finally made the trip from Evansville, Indiana, to Rockaway Beach to visit James at his home. They sat together at a small, circular table in the kitchen and drank cognac and smoked cigars.

They recalled the taste of C rations and the ruthless, bitter cold. They chuckled about stories like Pearson and the piano and about some of the more absurd moments, like the time McNulty mistook Hinson's foxhole for the latrine.

They also shared some things that they never had before. "Remember that farm girl you danced with, Jimmy, at the hall in La Crosse? Jesus, I forgot her name."

"Yeah," James said. "What about her?"

"Well, I never told you this," Leo began. "I don't know. I fig-ured maybe you'd get sore. But after I left you at the line for the telephone, I didn't go back to the dance hall like I said I was. I went to visit our friend down on the dairy farm."

James's face changed to one Leo was not familiar with. He was angry that Leo had waited all this time to tell him. Then he thought better of it and smiled.

"Well?" he asked. "Was it worth it?"

"Worth it?" Leo repeated with a toothy grin. "Let's just say I was picking hay out of my shorts for days."

Soon the linoleum tabletop was littered with photographs that Leo had taken so many years ago. There were pictures of the Queen Mary, which had taken them to Europe, and the bar-racks. There were candid shots of hedgerows, replacement de-pots, and the French Ardennes. And, of course, there were pictures of them. Young faces.

"Did we really look like that?" Leo asked.

Looking at the photographs, it was certainly hard to believe. To think that these young, vibrant boys had somehow morphed over time and were now trapped inside aging bodies, wrinkled and gray. How was it possible?

James watched curiously as Leo arranged the photographs in front of them like pieces from a jigsaw puzzle: Neil Hinson, Daniel Erikson, Patrick McNulty, Carmine Azzaro. It was as if the contents of his mind had been emptied and placed right before him.

He lifted a picture of John Sullivan from the table. He ex-plained to Leo how he still felt guilty about what happened that day at the outpost, how he could have and probably should have done more.

"It's always there, Leo," he explained. "You know what I mean?" Leo blew a mouthful of smoke into the heavy air and said that there were many things that he too regretted.

"It is what it is, Jimmy." There was nothing else to say.

James continued to sift through Leo's pictures. He removed a photograph from the pile that did not belong with the others, a color shot taken years after the war.

"What's this, Leo?" he inquired.

"U.S. cemetery, at Omaha Beach, Jimmy. I took it last year."

James's eyes followed the long, symmetrical rows of white grave markers that rolled across a lush, manicured blanket of green. It sent chills up his back. His first impulse was to put it down, to bury it beneath all the others. But he was intrigued. He couldn't put it down.

John, who happened to be in town that weekend on business, came into the room with Madeline and an armful of groceries. James did not look up, just continued to talk to Leo while studying the picture. Madeline went into the other room. John set the bags down on the counter and glanced in the direction of the two men. Leo acknowledged John with a half smile. John smiled back and walked over behind James.

"Wow, that's some picture, Dad?" he said. He had never seen anything like it.

"Sure is," he answered, without ever turning his head to face his son.

"Hello," John said, holding his hand out to Leo. "I'm John, James's son."

"Nice to meet you, John. Chris Leonardo. You probably know me as Leo."

"Right. That I do."

James finally turned to face John. "Why don't you sit down and join us, Johnny? Leo's got some great stories."

"I'd like to," he said, groping in his jacket pocket for his keys. "But I have something I need to take care of."

The air in the kitchen grew heavy. James turned back around. He frowned and looked off to the side a moment. Then his attention returned to the picture.

There was something different about that picture. It wasn't just the color. There was something else that seemed to step out of the image and grab him by the shirt collar. It was all so orderly and neat. It was contained. It made him marvel at how so much time and space and suffering and memory could be wrapped up so neatly in these countless rows of sparkling white.

He was suddenly aware of all the mess that filled his head. He wondered if he could clean it out, wrap it up nice and neat, the same way the photograph had done.

He liked the photographs. All of them. Their existence made everything more manageable. They allowed him to focus on the past, one frame at a time. That was all he could handle.

"These pictures are great, Leo," he said. "All of mine are locked away in the attic."

He wished he could take snapshots of all the rest of it, all the clutter from the past. He wished he could open up his head and get it out, all of it, frame by frame in a series of photographs that he could sort, arrange, order, and ultimately separate from the rest of himself. That's what he needed. Distance. Just a little room to step back and look.

"What was it like, Leo?" he asked. "I mean being back there? How did it feel?"

"It was strange, Jimmy. If I sat and stared long enough, I would've sworn I was right back."

It seemed tiring to him, but he wondered what it would be like. He thought about visiting. Perhaps a fresh look at things that were old and jumbled would allow him to order the chaos, to snap a picture of each floating piece of the past and consolidate each of the fragments into a small, neat little corner of his mind.

He thought back to his earliest days of war and about maybe visiting the outpost that the Germans had overrun on that horrible day. Maybe he'd sit there for a while and think about all that happened. He'd go over in his mind everything that Sully told them the night before. He'd remember the sound of the Germans in the next room and the call to Captain Swinton and the smell of sulfur and blood. Maybe he would lie down again, in the very same place where he had done so many years before, and finally understand that it was really the only thing he could have done. He'd hear the screams and the cries and the footsteps on gravel. This time it might finally make sense to him. The thought was fleeting.

It was probably not even there anymore. And if it were, it was most likely different now. It belonged to someone else, someone who probably knew nothing of the war and all that had happened. Probably a young mother with dirty-blonde hair pulled back off her face in a neat little bun. He pictured himself on her front steps and her coming to the door dressed in a blue apron with white ducks or kittens on the front, peeking through the unmistakable residue of her most recent domestic endeavor. What would she say to him? What would she think if he walked inside and lay down on the spot again, the same way he had done years before? She would never understand.

He considered going back to the road in Paderborn just over the flagstone bridge. He thought he might like to talk to the young German who stumbled innocently into him and Pearson one day while they were on scouting patrol. There were things, he thought, he'd like to ask him, like what it was he was writing that day while sitting helplessly at their feet. He wanted to know how he had become separated from the rest of his platoon. He thought he'd like to know his name. He wanted to explain to him that he never forgot his face and how he always felt that he had captured himself that day.

He wanted to say he was sorry. But the thought was transitory. He could re-create the entire scene. He could stand on that very spot where he stood before. He could feel the wet fog against his face and could ask as many questions as he liked. The truth was, there'd be no one there to answer.

He also fantasized about looking for the little German girl with the blonde hair. What would she look like? he wondered. He could locate the town where he had first seen her. That would be easy. He could stand in the street and trace her very last steps before she slipped into the distance with the elderly stranger. He could walk through every surrounding town and village, looking for those eyes. But when all was said and done, he considered how he would know—really know—who she was? She was an old woman by now, probably married with children and grandchildren of her own. Maybe she had managed to put the war behind her, to leave the painful image of her grandmother among the scattered debris in the littered street. Maybe she looked just like every other woman her age. How would he ever find her?

He thought for a second that maybe he wouldn't have to find her. Maybe she would remember him after all these years. Maybe she would pass him on the street and recognize the pain behind his eyes and somehow call back from the most remote regions of her memory that awful day in the littered street. Maybe she would remember, but it wasn't likely. He frowned and slid the pictures back across the table.

James got up and removed something from a cabinet adjacent to the sink on the other side of the room. "Does this look familiar?" he asked, placing an empty whiskey bottle in front of Leo.

"How the hell did you get that, Jimmy?" Leo asked, smiling.

"Hey. I got it once before, didn't I?" he joked.

"Let's see," Leo responded playfully. "I think it went something like 'Damn! There's nothing like good old American whiskey!' How'd I do?"

They both laughed.

John heard the laughter and stopped before heading out. He stood there, jingling the keys in his pocket.

"What's so funny?" he asked.

It got real quiet. The smile melted from James's face.

"What?" John asked.

"Never mind, Johnny," James grunted, shaking his head. "You wouldn't understand."

Tim Pearson was one of those guys they never got tired of talking about. James told Leo all about the "Dear John" Pearson received just three days before he was sent home. How it nearly killed him. He still remembered the vacant expression on Pearson's face as he packed his things and left without even a simple "see ya around." It was the same expression he noticed when he saw him again, years later, working one of the toll booths at the George Washington Bridge. Leo just shook his head.

Most of the others had faired much better. They had all gone on to live quiet lives in every corner of the country they served. Leo became a high school math teacher. Michael, the company runner, graduated from medical school first in his class. Although he never attended any of the reunions, Leo heard from a mutual friend that Dr. Michael Simmons had recently been appointed chief of staff at a university hospital in Texas. Peter Swinton became a bank manager. Crazy Jerry bought a dairy farm in the tiny town of Chateaugay, New York, and Carmine Azzaro opened what all the newspapers in Boston called the finest Italian restaurant in the entire New England area.

James and Leo continued to sift through the pile of photographs. Leo came across one of Patrick McNulty. They laughed.

"Remember Twitch?" James mused. "What a piece of work." The mere mention of McNulty's name lightened the mood. Of all the stories they had heard about postwar experiences, none was as comically absurd as the bizarre path that McNulty's life took.

After the war, McNulty began working as a baggage handler at a small airport in the Midwest and attending college at night. His time in and around the airport led to the idea that he could make a career there. Baggage handling soon became a drag. McNulty had set his sights higher, attaching his dreams to the massive tower that watched over the three runways of the tiny airfield. Air traffic control—it became his passion.

His employment as baggage handler and his extensive study in aviation somehow translated into the position in the tower that he had dreamed of for years. When his former buddies first heard about it, they were dumbfounded.

"Have these people actually met McNulty?" they joked. It was a scream. Something out of a Marx Brothers' movie. Patrick "Twitch" McNulty, the most neurotic, unstable man they had ever met, directing air traffic. How was it possible? What's next? they wondered. A Nobel Peace Prize for Tim Pearson?

When Leo was ready to leave, however, the tone of the visit turned solemn once again. "Are things any better with Johnny?" he asked. "Last letter you sent didn't sound so good."

"Ah, things are pretty much the same," James said. "I don't know, Leo. We just don't understand each other."

"You know, Jimmy. I met some guy recently at the VFW just down the road from my house. Reminded me of you a little. A typical dogface, unable to get over the war. He said a lot of things that made sense."

James grew indignant. "Look Leo," he said. "I'm glad things are good for you. Really. But the two of us are not the same. Never were."

"I know that, Jimmy. All I'm saying is that—"

"I know what you're saying," James insisted. He stood up and opened the refrigerator door. He stood there, his back to Leo, surveying the contents of every shelf. It was quiet, except for the tapping of Leo's foot against a table leg. James reached for a bottle of water and returned to his seat.

"I am not you, Leo," he said quietly. "That's all there is to it."

SEVENTEEN

★

They sat in the front row. The lighting was poor. The smell of carnations and orchids and other flowers perfumed the air. It was heavy and sweet, like someone had just emptied the contents of one of those canned air fresheners.

Two plastic easels holding cardboard placards tattooed with pictures that chronicled the life just lost attenuated the cold, dimly lit panels of the casket. That's how John knew her, not the way she looked now. Carrying Christmas cookies; smiling, as she helped her grandson blow out candles on his birthday cake; dancing with James at their anniversary party. Not like this.

They were all there. Together. The three McCleary boys. Their wives. All nine grandchildren. Others would be there

shortly. For Madeline. And for James. They saw he was strug-
gling. They wanted to help. All morning they made overtures.
Tried to soften the moment for him. But James was unavailable.
He had not said a word to any of them all morning.

John watched as the funeral director made last-minute ad-
justments to the room. Extra chairs for the back row. Tissue
boxes on each table. A fresh page for the guest book and a basket for mass cards. He wondered why anyone would ever choose
death as his livelihood. It was so depressing.

"Mrs. Fillmore called yesterday," Matt whispered to John.
"She said she'd help if we need anything."

He nodded his head. "How's Stephanie?" he asked. "Did she
hear?"

"Yeah," Matt said. "She'll probably be by later on tonight."

John grabbed his wife's hand and squeezed gently. Paul
leaned past her, catching John's attention.

"Do you see what I'm talking about?" he asked, motioning to
James, who was wrestling with the area just below his right
armpit. "He put them in his shirt yesterday." All three watched
from a distance.

"It's really weird," Paul continued. Matt nodded.

"I'm really worried about him," Matt agreed. "What the hell
are we going to do with him?"

★

Ovarian cancer. The doctors said they caught it in time. A
trip to her regular physician for some discomfort in her stomach. She had first noticed it a few weeks before, after a walk she
and James had taken in the park. Now she was on her way to a
specialist.

When she left that morning, she kissed him on the cheek and reminded him about their plans for the evening. "Now remember, Jimmy. We're going out with the Murphys tonight. Don't eat too much while I'm gone. She smiled and told him she loved him.

She came home later that afternoon with a look he had never seen before. "James," she said. "I have something to tell you."

Less than a month later, James was by her side at Sloan Kettering, feeding her Jell-O and dabbing her forehead with a damp cloth. She was pale. Her mouth pasty. Three rounds of chemo had robbed her of her hair and altered the map of her face. Still, he saw her the way he always had: young, beautiful.

*

He was always there. Each morning, he'd arrive just as the sun was pushing up over the skyscraper outside her window, flooding the room with warm rays of light. They would share breakfast, usually cold cereal and canned peaches or perhaps a bagel from the coffee shop across the street when time permitted. He would read to her, and she would doze. Late afternoon, he watched, with a feigned interest, her favorite soap operas. He learned most of the characters' names and indulged her affinity for talking about them as if they were real. She would doze off, again. She slept a lot. More, he thought, than was normal. It made the days seem much longer. He would not leave, though, for fear of not being right there when she awoke.

"Come on, Mr. McCleary," the nurses admonished him. "Go home and get some rest." He stayed. Just sat in his chair and watched the evening's steady approach, the sun withdrawing from her room, leaving everything inside shrouded in dying shadows.

She slept at odd intervals. This pushed him even harder to engage her during those few moments when she was lucid.

"They're redoing part of the boardwalk," he told her. "Down by the pier. I was over there yesterday. You wouldn't even recognize it. Looks good."

She smiled. "What about our secret spot, Jimmy?" she asked. "Remember? I hope they didn't do anything with that."

"Nah, I'm sure it's still there."

"Because," she continued, "you never know when we're gonna need it again."

They both laughed. The touch of his hand was warm and soft against hers.

"Now that's what I like to hear," he said.

"What? You didn't think you were going to get rid of me that easily, did you?"

They laughed even harder.

It was this laughter that struck John when he was in Manhattan attending a convention not too far from the hospital. He made the trip, flowers in hand, unannounced.

The smell of antiseptic bothered his nose. He stood outside her room, listening to his father's playful banter and easy laughter. They were sounds he had never heard before. The voice of a stranger. He was tempted to stand there a little longer. But a quick glance at his watch curbed the impulse.

"Hey, gorgeous," he said to her. "How are you feeling?"

"Oh, Jonathan," she said. "They're beautiful. What a wonderful surprise."

His father's mood changed the moment he saw him. He

stopped talking. He let Madeline's hand fall to the side and took a seat on the other side of the room, by the window.

When John left, he stopped by the nurses' station. He must have been caught in the tumult that defined the shift change, for it was several minutes before anyone even acknowledged him. He stood there, still trying to reconcile the sound of his father's laughter with the man it belonged to. Finally, one of the nurses who had been flipping through patient charts looked up at him.

"How's my mother doing?" he asked. "Madeline McCleary?"

"Your mother is a very sick lady, Mr. McCleary," she said.

John frowned.

"Is there anything we can do?" he asked. "To make it a little easier for her?"

"Your father has already done that," she told him. "He is a remarkable man, your dad. He is here every day. Talks with her. Feeds her. I mean, it is the most . . . well, I don't have to tell you. He's your father. It's just really special. All of the nurses on the floor are talking about it."

*

People began filing into the room and past the casket. Neighbors. Cousins. Distant relations. There were many faces from John's past, faces he had not seen in years or cared to see now. He was suddenly warm and uncomfortable with the closeness.

He shot out of his chair. He walked off to the side and surveyed the photo collages his wife and sister-in-law had helped put together. The suffocation grew worse. He realized that it was part of a larger sensation, the feeling that a whole sequence of his life had been expunged. She was his past, so much a part of who he had become. What would happen now?

He tried to recall her life, year by year, but time was no longer hands scraping across the face of a clock. Time was the kitchen, hair curlers, her crossword puzzles, and that smile. She was always so happy. That smile. It was what he loved most about her. The warm smile and remarkable resiliency behind it.

"Can I ask you something, Mom?" he asked. The waitress had just seated the two of them in a booth by the window.

"How did you and Dad meet?"

"At a grocery store, Jonathan," she said. "The A & P where he worked. You've heard the adage 'love at first sight'? Well, that was it."

"Really?" John asked.

"Don't look so surprised, Jonathan. Your father wasn't always the man you see now."

"Yeah. Sure."

"I'm serious," she said. "We walked on the beach, held hands in the movie theater. He used to sing in my ear when we danced. I have to say he was quite a romantic."

John ripped open a tiny Styrofoam container of half-and-half and stirred it into his coffee. The white swirls spun around like strands of cotton until they disappeared beneath the surface.

"I'll tell you something, Jonathan," she said. "Something that you do not know. The night your father asked me to marry him was the happiest one of my life."

"I can just imagine. Did he get on one knee and pledge his undying love for you," he mocked, tapping the edges of his cup with a spoon.

"Don't be a smart aleck, Jonathan McCleary. It was nothing like that at all. We sat on the edge of the pier, staring out at the sunset over Jamaica Bay. He had his arm around me and was playing with my hair. All of a sudden he started telling me this story—he made it up, right there—about a little boat we had both been watching out on the water." Her voice was gentle and hopeful. She detailed the moment as if it had just happened yesterday.

"He was like that boat," he said to me. "Lost, struggling against the tide. Then he told me that I came along and pulled him to shore. Then he kissed me and he . . . he reached into his pocket, grabbed my hand, and slipped a beautiful ring on my finger."

Her voice trailed off as she completed the reminiscence. She lifted a napkin to her eyes. "Pretty amazing, huh?" she asked.

John shook his head. Who was she talking about? He turned to face the window. For a minute, his gaze was fixed on the scene outside. A German shepherd had wandered into the middle of the road and stopped the flow of traffic. A couple of people had left their cars and were trying to guide the dog to the sidewalk, yelling to it over the discord of horns.

These were the worst moments for him, when he had enough time to think. Was his father the distant, callous son of a bitch he always thought him to be? Or was it rather him?

"What happened to him, Mom?" he asked.

"What happened?" she repeated. All of a sudden she looked angry.

"Plenty, Jonathan. He was away a long time. A lot happened."

He wasn't exactly sure what that meant or how it had anything to do with what he had asked.

"I never liked the way he talked to you," he explained. "Or any of us. Like we were intruding on him or something. It drove me crazy. How did you do it, Mom? All these years."

"It wasn't all bad, Jonathan," she said. "There were good times too. Many of them. And when you love someone, you remember the good and hope that one day you'll see it again."

She had always entertained the thought that somehow the father and son would find a way. Listening to him now, she realized the improbability of such an idea.

"You are so angry, Jonathan," she said. "Why don't you tell me exactly what bothers you so much. You harbor things, Jonathan. Just like him. It's not healthy."

"I don't know if I can explain it."

"Try."

He leaned forward and folded his hands on the table. "This might sound weird, but remember that spinning game we used to play when we were little?" he began. "You know, spin yourself around until you can barely stand up anymore?"

"Remember it?" She laughed. "How could I forget it? I patched more knees because of that silly game."

He had shredded his napkin and was beginning to place all the pieces into his empty cup. She was impatient, waiting for him to finish what he was saying. "What does that game have to do with what I asked you?" she said.

John talked nostalgically about the hours spent spinning on the lawn in front of their house. How he would corkscrew across the grass, arms outstretched, head thrown back and to the side, watching as everything whizzed by in a dizzying streak of color, one image melting into the next, like a giant outdoor kaleidoscope. And then the desperate attempt to follow the curb that ran along the street, wobbling precariously while willing himself not to stumble.

"I loved that game," he explained, "for the very same reason I drank so much later on. And smoked. It blurred everything. Made it all bearable somehow. I used to play that game any time something bothered me."

John tried to describe for her the rush he felt, the reordering of the universe as seen through eyes in motion. It was new and exciting, full of improbability. Until, of course, the dizziness subsided and everything regained focus. The altered consciousness always gave way to painful lucidity, opened up like a sudden separation of clouds, a flood of light cast onto scenes of austere absence.

"It was my escape, Mom," he continued. "I was a stupid kid. As I got older, I stopped. But I looked for substitutes. That was childish too. But that feeling never left. That feeling of wanting to slip out of the misery never left."

"I'm sorry you feel that way, Jonathan," she said. "It hurts me to hear it. But you need to understand. We've had this talk before. Your father . . . he has had some bad experiences."

He was looking out the window again. The German shepherd was gone. "I know. I know, Mom. I've heard it all before," he complained. "But if this story of his is so important, so vital to me understanding who he is, then why don't you just tell me about it. Tell me the story."

"I can't do that, Jonathan," she replied. "I do not know it well enough. And even if I did, I wouldn't. It's not mine to tell."

EIGHTEEN

✯

James sits quietly by the window, while John continues his assault on the attic. He hears his son's cell phone ring several more times and wonders who he's talking to. As he tries to figure out the muffled words falling from up above, his thoughts skip back in time, making all their usual stops.

Six thousand miles separated James from the abandoned buildings and grassy, mine-laden fields. He was different now. Distant and stoic. He had assumed another life in the small, tree-lined suburban neighborhood where he and Madeline had settled. He was a pharmacist and she a homemaker. They vacationed every year upstate with their three children. They were

both very active in the church as well. He had become a grandfather.

But it was all still so real. The pungent odor of sulfur. The
taste of blood and the ceaseless reverberations of metal piercing metal. The tank tracks in the mud and snipers on rooftops.
The unmistakable feeling of sand in your boots and cold, gray
drizzle on your face. The burden of survival, the unfulfilled vow
that they would all come home together. And of course, there
was always the image of the man he captured.

Fifty-six years and six thousands miles. But sitting in his
house, staring out a window while thinking of his wife and those
boxes upstairs, James is again face-to-face with the young German soldier he and his partner Tim Pearson captured during a
routine scouting patrol on a foggy day in the town of Paderborn.

It was James's first real look at the enemy. They had been assigned to secure a flagstone bridge on the west side of the village. The German soldier, separated from his company and
disoriented, ran right into them.

"Take his weapon and his pack," grunted Pearson.

The young German was stunned. He struggled to say something. Out of the hysteria and terror came the barely audible
words "stop," "peace," and "Uncle Sam."

Pearson chuckled. He made the prisoner remove his helmet. "Hey, Nazi boy," he taunted. "Heil Hitler."

The young German did not respond. Pearson knocked him
to his knees. The German boy's voice was again tremulous and
weak. "Stop, peace, Uncle Sam," he repeated.

He writhed quietly, his hands folded together, praying hard
for deliverance as Pearson circled him, assaulting him with in-

vectives. Fifty-six years later, the images that flitted before James were just as vivid: the tears that created such a peculiar pattern as they slid down the dirty cheeks of the prisoner; the spasmodic breathing of the young German; the quivering of his lower lip each time Pearson glared into his dark, forlorn eyes; the agitation. And then the desperate request for his pack.

To a soldier, the pack was life. It was a conduit to the past, filled with little pieces of the world he left behind. It was his only comfort when his own death appeared imminent. James and Pearson were aware of the possible dangers that could lie concealed in a soldier's pack. There was always talk of hidden grenades or pistols, though they had never actually seen any. Still, to be safe, they spilled the contents of the pack on the ground and took a quick survey of the items: five wrinkled pieces of tan paper and a pen, photographs of a beautiful girl slid between the pages of a tattered black prayer book, an empty canteen, a pipe, and a variety of religious articles.

They returned the pack. There was no danger there.

The young German soldier began to write feverishly, while Pearson began to talk of commendations, of being decorated for capturing the enemy. "This is good, Jimmy boy," he boasted. "Real good."

James did not hear a word he said. He was fixated on the prisoner, following the erratic movements of his pen, repeating to himself the contents of the pack: photographs of a young, beautiful girl; black prayer book; religious articles; keepsake.

Pearson continued his awkward display of bravado. "What should we do with the kraut's note?" he asked, ripping the paper from the prisoner's quivering hand. James was quiet. He grabbed the paper from Pearson. "Ease up, Pearson," he told him.

The note was written in German and James could not understand most of what it said. But it was damp with pain and passion. It bothered him to look at it. He folded it up and stuffed it in his pocket.

He remembered training camp at Fort Custer and the teachings of Sergeant Billings. He recalled vividly the pictures that all of the recruits were shown.

"This is the enemy," Billings always said, gnashing his teeth. "He is a cold, vicious, killing machine."

Now James sat with his elbows resting on his knees, struggling to make sense of this new reality. The enemy looked very different up close, a far cry from the demoniac, callous abstraction Billings had shown him. He was not a fiend. He was no monster. James recognized that the enemy looked, oddly enough, just like him: a young kid, scared and bewildered. He missed his mother and father. He loved his sweetheart. He had the same fear of death that all soldiers possessed. This made him sad.

He was thinking of his own pack and the things he carried: a picture of his girlfriend, Madeline, sitting under the boardwalk at Rockaway Beach; rosary beads; letters from home held together by a dirty shoelace; a plastic Mickey Mouse he had won at Coney Island. There was no denying it; he had captured himself.

And exactly how do you escape from yourself? Fifty-six years and six thousand miles; a wife and three children; a four-bedroom colonial in a small town just six blocks from the pharmacy he owned; nine grandchildren. But James was stuck in the Paderborn fog. He still wondered what it was the German soldier wrote and for whom it was intended. Was it a tearful farewell to his mother and father? A declaration of his eternal love for the beautiful girl in the picture? A condemnation of his captors?

When James returned to camp later that day, Chris Leonardo, his best friend in the company, was banging out field blankets with a wooden stick. He noticed James stumbling across the open area between the tents and called to him. "Hey McCleary? Why don't you give me a hand over here?" Leo called.

"What the heck happened to you?" James said, walking over to him. "I thought you had patrol with me?"

Leonardo told him how he earned this extra duty by mouthing off during inspection. James said nothing, just dropped his pack, picked up a stick and began whacking a blanket.

"So what's with you, Jimmy?" Leo asked. "You and Pearson find any krauts on patrol?"

"Yeah, Leo. One."

"Are you shittin' me? It just figures. Did you catch him?"

"Yup."

"Can I get a look at him? Where is he now?"

"Don't know," James said. "I left him with Pearson back at the bridge. But one of the replacements took a picture for Pearson. I'm sure he'll be happy to share."

Leo was furious with himself. He began to describe all the things he would have done to the German had he been there. James was silent. But he began to hit the blanket with more and more violent blows. Leo put his stick by his side and watched as James worked himself into a frenzy. His breathing was hard and forced. He was mumbling something that could not be understood. Sweat from his furrowed brow ran down the sides of his nose and mixed with some tears that had escaped from his eyes.

"Jesus Christ, McCleary! What the hell is wrong with you?" Leonardo grabbed him.

James whirled around, wielding the stick over his head. "Get the hell off me, goddamn you! Get off me!"

Leonardo backed off. "Holy shit, McCleary! Take it easy. Relax. Go sit down somewhere."

James walked away quietly. Leonardo just shook his head. "It's alright, fellas," Leonardo said to the other soldiers who had gathered. "Just stay away from him."

James went off by himself and sat with his pack on his lap. He pulled the German's note from his pocket, then stuffed it back into his pack and took out some blank sheets of paper of his own.

"*Dear Maddie . . .* "

When Pearson got back, he explained to the others what had happened. He said that the young soldier had tried to escape. Everyone knew that was a lie.

James always regretted the decision to keep the note. But he didn't know what else to do. Now he wished he had done anything but that. It stayed there for the duration of the war. It was still there. It frightened him.

NINETEEN

⋆

The three McCleary boys and their father crowd around a small table in the kitchen. The two white boxes from Gino's Pizzeria and a two-liter bottle of Pepsi that sit quietly on the counter behind them make up the contents of what is to become their last dinner together in the house.

"I'll finish up here tomorrow morning," John says. "Everything should be out of the house by lunchtime. Are you all set at your place, Matty?"

He places one of the boxes on the table and opens the top. The smell of tomato sauce and pepperoni fills his nostrils. Matt struggles with the plastic wrapper covering a stack of paper plates.

"Yup," he says, tearing one of the corners of the wrapper with his teeth. "A fresh coat of paint on the walls. New bed frame. Dad saw the room yesterday and loved it. You like the room, right Dad? Dad?"

James is bending the edges of his plate with his fingers. He is thinking about the first time he showed Madeline the house. It was winter. She was wearing a black coat with a fur collar. Her cheeks were still rosy from the biting January winds. She couldn't stop smiling. Then she cried and told him it was perfect, the home she always dreamed of.

"Sure," he says.

John places a couple of slices of pizza and some garlic knots on his plate. He has been eating ravenously since he got there last week. He was so hungry all the time, like he was hollow inside. He just kept shoveling it in. But it appeared no amount of food would satisfy the emptiness.

"Hey, when is that realtor coming by again, Johnny?" Paul asks. "I've a got a friend at work who'd like to ask her a few questions."

"She'll be here tomorrow," John says. "I'm seeing her at twelve-thirty to finalize some paperwork and then I'm hopping a cab to LaGuardia right after that. My flight leaves at three."

The air in the kitchen grows slowly oppressive.

"Hard to believe, eh Pauly?" Matt says. He unscrews the cap on the Pepsi bottle and pours deliberately.

"Yeah. I hear you," Paul answers. "Strange to think of anyone else sitting here, you know? He turns to James. "Dad, you sure you don't want a slice? he asks.

James shakes his head. He is content to just sit there, fingering the edges of the plate.

"You really should eat, Pop," John insists, placing a piece of pizza in front of the vacant old man.

"Johnny," Paul says, eager to divert the course of conversion. "Are you gonna sleep here tonight, or do you want to stay by me?"

"I was sort of thinking that we'd all stay here," John says. "You know, one last time?"

Paul and Matthew look uncomfortably at each other.

"Listen, Johnny," Matt says. "Paul and I already talked about this. The last time we did that it didn't work out so well."

"Hey, that's fine," John responds. "No sweat, really."

John reaches into the box. He folds a slice of pizza into a triangle and bites down hard.

"I have an idea, Johnny," Matt says. "Why don't you stay with Pauly, at his place, and I'll get Dad settled in his new room."

"No, no. I think I'll stay right here," he answers. "I want to. Besides, I have some things to take care of."

"What about you, Dad?" Matt asks. "Do you want to stay, or do you want to come by me?"

James does not stir. His eyes are lost in the grooves of the pale wood wainscoting on the walls in front of him. In his ears are faint voices, distant and muffled.

"Dad? Hey, Dad," he repeats, placing his hand on James's shoulder. "Do you want to stay with me tonight?"

"No. It's not necessary. I'm good here," he says. "I'm good. I'll stay here."

"We'll be fine here, Matt," John insists. "Really. I'll finish up packing and finalize things with the realtor in the morning. Then I'll drop Dad by your place before I leave."

★

John lies flat, hands locked behind his head, staring at the tarnished chain of beads that hangs from the ceiling fan above. The room is all but empty, with the exception of the twin bed on which he rests and the lamp and alarm clock that sit nakedly on a milk crate that doubles as a nightstand. Presently, his thoughts are limited to the remaining details germane to the sale of the house: real estate paperwork, a phone call to the utility companies, a couple of overstuffed cardboard boxes that need to be dragged to the curb, his father's army pack, and the pile of letters.

When he closes the light, he finds himself wrestling with thoughts of a more haunting nature. The years he spent in the house unfurl before him, a series of ghostlike images that flicker in the darkness. Most of these are unpleasant, and he swats at them with erratic blinks of his eyes. He is certain there are good times to recall, but they just won't come. He is frustrated. Maybe this is how memories work, he laments. The brain has only a limited capacity to house these scenes from the past. So, you hold onto only those that have made the deepest impressions. It is this thought that trails him for hours until he finally drifts off.

He awakens the following morning with a dull ache that stretches across his forehead and behind his eyes. He grabs some Motrin and a couple of swallows of Pepsi before making his final trip to the attic.

James sits quietly below on the only piece of furniture remaining, the old brown chair by the window.

John is tired. He stacks a bunch of empty boxes and slides them over to the attic door. It is virtually empty. It looks a lot bigger now. Strange. There is not much left on the dusty floor. Just an old pile of clothes, ready for the curb, and a few odds and ends he needs to put somewhere. And his father's pack. He hasn't decided what to do with it.

He sits down, one last time, and continues to sift through the contents. He finds a few more pictures of James and his buddies and an empty pack of Lucky Strikes. Underneath are a few bottle caps and some foreign coins. He holds each of the objects in his hand briefly, imagining James's hands on them many years before. Then he places them next to the stack of letters he has set aside. He is disappointed. It appears that he has found all there is to find.

With some reluctance, he tosses the empty pack onto the pile of clothes. The outside flap falls open, and a sheet of paper slips out. He bends to pick it up. It is a note, written in German.

The wrinkled sheet of paper is old and tattered and yellowing with time. Fifty-six years have passed since James buried it there. Now, exposed once more to the light, there is no denying the anguish in the scribbled lines.

John is confused at first. He doesn't understand. A German letter? In his father's pack? It doesn't make sense. He begins to translate each line.

The reading is difficult. He is fluent in the language, but the writing is sloppy and some of the words have been smeared. He struggles and considers putting it aside, but he is far too intrigued to walk away.

The man who wrote the note was Franz Hogenmiller. He was seventeen years old at the time, the youngest soldier in the

116th Panzer Division. Before he was a soldier, he lived with his
mother and five younger brothers above Zausins Bakeshop, a
small brick building in a town miles from Paderborn where he
and the entire division were dug in, awaiting the arrival of the
Americans.

He was nervous. He had never fired his weapon. And the
thought of facing the Americans scared him like nothing else.
Horrible thoughts filled his head.

"The American is your enemy," the German commander
told all of them. "He is a cold, vicious killing machine." He was
not ready for war. He was young. He carried things in his pack
that he hoped would make him feel better: pictures of his girl; a
prayer book; a small, fur-covered terrier dog with glass eyes, just
like the one waiting for him back home; some paper for writing
letters. Franz was not really a soldier.

He was still thinking about waking up each morning to the
smell of cinnamon and warm bread when one of the officers approached him.

"Franz, you stay here. You will be lookout."

The rest of the division retreated. They would wait for
Franz's signal.

An hour passed. No sign of the Americans. He sat in a shell
hole, eyes fixed on a point in the distance. Thoughts of home
and his girlfriend, Gerty, helped fill the idle time. He was remembering the first time the two of them snuck off to be with
each other. They were just fourteen. Gerty's parents were
adamant about her not seeing Franz. "You are too young," her
father commanded. "Boys like this one are trouble."

But her father's edict was no match for the warm spring

breeze and the smell of honeysuckle and the first discovery of love.

They rendezvoused behind the Mueller's barn. "We can't stay here Gerty. Someone will see."

She smiled and stroked his worried face. "Don't worry, Franz," she said. "Please. Only smiles."

"But where can we go, Gerty?" he asked her nervously.

"I know a place," she told him. "Let's walk to the stream, past the hills on the other side of the woods."

It was just as they both had pictured. Peaceful and quiet, except for the sound of water rushing across the rocks sticking up out of the muddy bed. They found two boulders that were flat and sat down beside each other. Soon they had taken off their shoes and were laughing as the cool water tickled their toes.

"Franz," she said softly to him. "I don't care what Papa says. I love you."

"I love you too, Gerty," he told her. Then he leaned over to her and closed his eyes. The cool water on his feet and the warmth of her lips on his was magical. It was their first kiss.

In an instant, the sound of falling shells and machine gun fire shattered the daydream. He could hear the distant cries of his comrades behind him as they retreated, struggling with an attack that had come unexpectedly. He was paralyzed with indecision.

He waited. The explosions lasted several minutes. Each one drove him deeper into his hole. He trembled. He did not want to be alone, but he was too afraid to leave. He counted the second between each blast, trying to figure out the best time to run. The pattern was too erratic.

It is no use, he realized. I am stuck.

He waited for hours. He sat still, alone with his thoughts. When the shelling stopped, he lifted his head and peered warily out across the ruins. An eerie silence slipped out of the smoke billowing from the battered town. He climbed from the hole and began his attempt to find the others.

He was uncertain which way to go. He had never been good with navigation. Woodworking. That was his specialty. It was what he loved most.

He followed the path they all had traveled together only hours before, but nothing looked familiar. He turned right and walked a few steps. Then he did the same in the other direction. He did the same thing two more times. Minutes later, he was standing on the very same spot where he started.

He turned in the direction of the smoke and sighed. He decided that this must be the way. Up ahead, through a screen of smoke and fog, he could see the outline of a flagstone bridge that connected the road he was following with the Paderborn village. He smiled. This was where his division was stationed.

He was halfway across the bridge when he came face-to-face with two figures that had suddenly stepped out of the fog: American soldiers on scouting patrol. Franz was stunned. His eyes filled with tears, and his legs began to tremble.

"Take his weapon and his pack," one said to the other. Franz held his hands above his head.

"Stop— peace— Uncle Sam—" he muttered.

The one called Pearson laughed. He made Franz remove his helmet.

"Hey, Nazi boy," he said to him. "Heil Hitler."

Franz did not respond. Pearson laughed again and knocked him to his knees.

"Stop— peace— Uncle Sam—" he repeated, praying that the angry American would show mercy.

The other American was quiet. Franz saw pity in his eyes. He hoped he could help. Franz held out his arms in his direction, begging for his pack. It was safe in his hands once both of the Americans emptied its contents on the ground. Franz took some sheets of paper from the pile and began to write.

★

John is unsteady as he walks down the stairs, the pack over his shoulder, letter in hand. James hears the sound of footsteps and turns in the direction of the intrusion.

"Where did you get that, Jonathan? Where did you get that?" he repeats desperately.

"It's okay, Dad," he says.

The young German's face appears before him, just as it did years ago. "Leave me alone," James says. It is all in front of him, all at once.

"It's okay, Dad," John repeats.

"No. No, Johnny. It's not. You had no right. You had no right to—"

John takes a few steps towards his father. His hands are trembling. He holds out the letter.

"You do not understand," James continues. "I did not want to. I never wanted to—"

"Dad, it's okay," he tells him again.

"It wasn't me, Jonathan," he pleads. "Wasn't me. You don't understand."

"Dad, listen to me. Do you know what this says?"

James is still. His eyes are glazed. Then he begins to cry and shakes his head no.

"Do you want to know?" John asks.

There is a long pause. Finally, he nods, and whispers softly, "Okay."

John reads:

Please tell my parents and my girl that I love them. They must know. Please. I curse this war. I think you understand. You are not like your friend, angry and scared. I do not blame you for what you do. I'd have done the same to you. Why did they have to lie to us?

Do not worry. I forgive you. One of us must die so that the other may live. That is war. I just hope you make something out of this opportunity. Someday, we'll meet again in a place where all of this will not matter.

Until then,

Franz Hogenmiller

James is on his knees, bowing before the spectral images that have begun to assemble on the altar of truth. He is looking down at the floor. He lifts his head to say something. Tears stream down his cheeks. John goes to him and helps him to his feet. The embrace is awkward at first, then warm and tender.

He watches as his father reaches into his shirt and pulls out a pair of white socks. He releases them to the ground in front of him.

"I miss your mother, Johnny," he whispers tearfully.

John looks down at the floor, then at his watch. They have less than an hour left in the house.

"I know, Dad," he says. "I know."

Accurst be he that first invented war.

—CHRISTOPHER MARLOWE

ACKNOWLEDGMENTS

✯

To my parents, especially my mother, whose courage and dignity will always be my greatest inspiration.

Eternal thanks to Steve Cohen, a special friend who believed in the integrity of this novel every step of the way.

Thank you to my early readers: Jennifer Weis, Tim Bent, Richie Woods, and Ron Ross.

To the most talented editor around, Joe Cleemann, whose patience, insight, passion, and creativity were most instrumental in bringing this story to life. Thank you, Joe. You are the best.

Much appreciation to my friend Steve Kohut for laying the groundwork for the Veterans Speaker Program at Oceanside

High School, something that became the inspiration for this book.

Thank you to Ken Belfield for his historical expertise.

To my friends and colleagues Frank Luisi, Nancy Padgett, and Sheryl Rubin. Thank you for your contributions, support, and encouragement.

For having the courage to share memories from a past that is both private and painful, thank you, Ed Hynes and Bill McGinn.

To my special little boys, Nicholas and Anthony. I know it wasn't easy, but we made it. Thank you for sharing your daddy.

And of course to my beautiful wife, Julia, whose love and devotion have lifted me to heights of unimaginable proportions. Thank you, Jules. I love you.